215

My Name Is Not
Angelica

My Name Is Not Angelica

Scott O'Dell

A Yearling Book

Published by
Dell Publishing
a division of
Bantam Doubleday Dell Publishing Group, Inc.
666 Fifth Avenue
New York, New York 10103

ISBN: 0-440-40379-0

Reprinted by arrangement with Houghton Mifflin Company

Printed in the United States of America

October 1990

10 9 8 7 6 5 4 3 2 1

OPM

To Rosa Parks
who would not sit in the back of the bus

Author's Note

In the writing of *My Name Is Not Angelica,* I talked to librarians and teachers on the islands of St. Thomas and St. John and to the descendants of slaves who lived through the revolt of 1733–1734.

The island of St. John was discovered by Columbus in 1493. It passed from hand to hand among the Spaniards, the Dutch, the British, and the French until the year 1717, when it was settled by the Danes. Two hundred years later they sold the island to the United States.

Besides numerous scholarly papers, I found most helpful Westergaard's *The Danish West Indies Under Company Rule;* Jadan's booklet *A Guide to Natural History of St. John; Night of the Silent Drums* by John Anderson, who spent thirty-five years of research on this fine novel; and the splendid books of the explorer Basil Davidson, *Black Mother: The African Slave Trade, The African Genius,* and *The Lost Cities of Africa.*

ATLANTIC

OCEAN

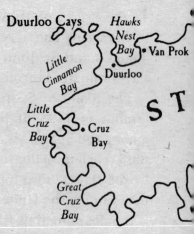

Whistli
Cay

Duurloo Cays

Hawks
Nest
Bay

Van Prok

Little
Cinnamon
Bay

Duurloo

S T

Little
Cruz
Bay

Cruz
Bay

ST.

THOMAS

Great
Cruz
Bay

N

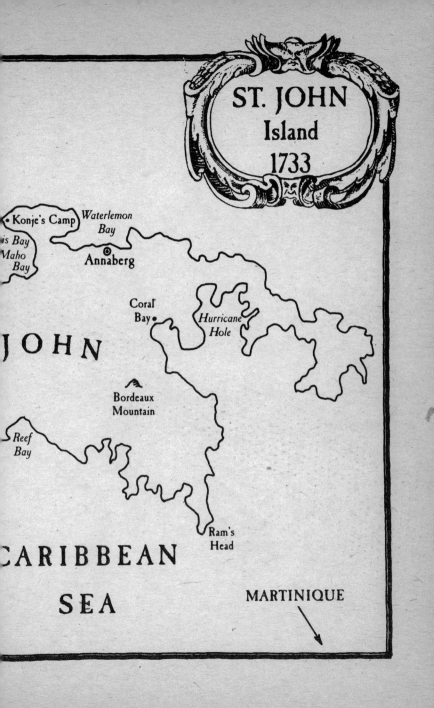

My Name Is Not
Angelica

1

Late in the summer King Agaja sent out ten of his five hundred women guards. They came down the river in a war canoe. They wore golden shifts, loops of moonstone beads, and silver rings, but each of them carried a cutlass.

I stood beside my father at the river's edge, holding my sister's hand. I was sixteen and tall for my age, but I felt like a child beside these giant women as they strode toward the ceiba tree where Konje waited. They looked like ten giant statues come to life.

The leader spoke to Konje in a queenly voice. "King Agaja," she said, "King of Zamboya, Emperor of Lands to the West and East, has learned of your father's death. The news has saddened His Majesty. He fears that the friendship between Zamboya and Barato will languish and die."

My father, Tembu Motara, the chief counselor of Barato, squeezed my hand as the word "friendship" was spoken. Never was there any friendship between King Agaja and Konje's father. No one in Barato had ever seen the king. His merchants had never traded with us.

The leader went on. "In order that this friendship will not end, His Majesty will give a feast ten days from this day, to which you and your court are invited."

Konje, who could smile at a charging lion, was startled when the ten warriors stepped from the canoe. He was startled when their leader spoke to him. He bowed twice, tugged at this belt, then glanced at my father.

In his deep voice, my father replied, "Please inform His Majesty that in the spirit of friendship we accept his generous invitation."

The leader, towering over us all, looking beyond us, said, "His Majesty will be pleased that he will have the good fortune to entertain you and your court."

Without more words, to the tinkling of bracelets, she led her warriors to the canoe and quietly they set off up the muddy river. She waved and the village waved back.

"The invitation surprises me. What do you think of it?" Konje asked my father.

"We go to the feast, of course. But before we go, we think hard. The flood has changed things. Barato is no longer six villages hidden in the wilderness, far from the river and the sea."

Last April, when it rained nights and days for

weeks, our mighty river changed its course. In a great loop, it rushed away from the country King Agaja ruled and left him without a harbor. The river's new course washed out one of our villages and most of our palm forest, but miraculously we were now on the sea.

"King Agaja has lost his harbor," my father said. "Now he has to send his goods through Barato. What's on his mind is very simple. He doesn't want to pay us a tax on the goods he'll ship, even a small tax."

Konje knew little about business. "What does the king send?"

"Elephant tusks, gold, palm oil. Also slaves."

"Slaves? From where?"

"From lands beyond the mountains where the river begins. But he collects them from everywhere. Each year he sends more than six thousand to Spain and Portugal. To other countries also."

"We cannot collect a tax on slaves," Konje said. "I do not like the idea."

"It's the most profitable tax of all. King Agaja would pay us a tax for every slave he sends out. And a tax on what he is paid in return — a musket, lead, and barrels of powder. You'll be rich in a short time."

"No," Konje said.

"You own slaves. I own slaves. All the elders own slaves. What's the difference between our slaves and those that King Agaja sends?"

3

"Ours are well treated, a part of the family. Of the slaves that are sold, I have heard, many are roasted over hot fires and eaten."

"Eaten?" my father exclaimed. "That's nonsense."

The sun was going down in a bank of rain clouds. A cool wind wandered in from the harbor. Servants came with a string of horses. It was the time of day when Konje and his lordly friends rode off to the grasslands, beyond the swamps and the palm forest that surrounded us, to hunt wildebeests and panthers.

The beribboned horses caught Konje's eye. He clapped his hands like a child and hummed a tune. He chose a beautiful spotted mare, leaped on her back, and began to circle the tree where my father and I stood. He rode slowly, sitting straight on his gold-trimmed blanket.

His eyes were fixed on me. He wanted to make sure that I was watching. I watched while he made two slow circles of the big ceiba tree. "Raisha, do you like the horse?" he said.

"It's beautiful," I said.

We would not be married until he was thirty years old. Now he was only twenty-seven. That was the law of Barato. It was never broken. He liked to tease me. Once I teased him. I hinted that one of the elders had asked me to marry. But both of us knew that our hearts were joined forever.

2

Days after the women warriors left, King Agaja sent canoes filled with flowers, with night-blooming cereus, pink jungle ferns, and frangipani. Our village ran down to the river to meet them.

Warriors, who spread the flowers under the ceiba tree, and a grizzled dwarf got out of the canoe. He waddled up the pathway and stood stiffly in front of Konje.

"Flowers of friendship," he said in a piping voice. "A gift from King Agaja to the women of your court."

Konje was startled at the sight. He couldn't think of anything to say. He had to do something to repay King Agaja. But what? He glanced at my father, who looked away, a signal meant to calm him. But Konje went on. He sent a servant to the counting house. The man came back with a gourd of river pearls that shone like the moon as it sets at the break of day.

"With pleasure I send King Agaja these pearls of friendship," Konje said.

The dwarf smiled showing gold teeth. "His Majesty will be pleased, also the women who will wear them." He pressed the pearls to his chest. "How many of your beautiful guests will we have?"

"Ninety-three from this village," Konje said. "From the other five villages, I don't know. It is harvest time with them."

He excused himself and went to a papa drum sitting among the trees, the big one made of a hollow log covered with goatskin. He beat on the drum with his hands and talked to the nearest village. Then he talked to the rest of the villages, beating the big drum with a rhinoceros horn.

Numbers came back quickly. He added them to the number from our village and told the dwarf that he would come to the feast with one hundred and eight guests, possibly a few more.

"As many as you wish," the dwarf said. "His Majesty has just given a month's shelter to a caravan from Ethiopia of more than two hundred merchants."

Konje ran a hand through his bushy hair. He frowned. Again he glanced at my father. I was sure that he wanted to make another gift. He had given pearls to the women of Agaja's court. Must he make a gift to King Agaja himself?

Again my father cast a cold eye at Konje and turned away. He was very careful with money. In a big book bound in zebra hide he put down all the money that came into and went out of our six villages. And as the chieftain of Barato, until the day Konje reached the age of thirty, he would keep a tight rope on the spoiled young man.

Rain began to fall. Warriors leaped out of the canoe and held mats over the dwarf, as if they thought he would melt away. He touched his forehead to the ground and bowed himself to the river. He faced Konje as he went, yet I noticed that he cast a long look at the bamboo wharf the Elders were building at the mouth of the river.

From his canoe, he called out, "In three days I will meet you at the gates of Malai, be it day or night."

True to his word, he was there three days later, wrapped in folds of scarlet cloth that sparkled with jewels, with two rows of naked guards that stretched from the river bank to an odd-shaped hill some distance beyond.

Up this pathway, between the two rows of guards glistening in the heat, the dwarf led the way. Konje walked behind him and the rest of us followed Konje. The sound of trumpets and little tan-tan drums came from somewhere.

On both sides of the path were streets straight as arrows faced with mud and straw huts, half of them in ruins. Men crowded the street, carrying stones.

Between the rows of guards, the pathway led

toward a stone cliff. Circles and triangles and zig-zag lines were painted on its face in glittering colors.

The pathway began to narrow. The top of the cliff turned outward and hung above us. We left the guards behind. Suddenly we were in a walled, cavelike place. The pathway went no farther. Over our heads was a glimpse of blue sky and a white cloud.

The dwarf, speaking in a gentle tone, placed us against a wall. A basket came down through the hole over our heads.

"We go up to the king's gardens and his palace," he said. "We go seven at a time. It is not far to the top."

But the top was far, high as ten men. There were more than a hundred guests, yet servants lowered the basket and pulled it up before the dwarf had finished telling Konje how many invaders had tried to climb the cliff and failed.

"Not just one cliff protects the king," he said. "Cliffs surround the palace on every side. Most of the invaders are slain at the river. Those who reach this far go no farther."

While the basket went up and down, he told us tales of those who had foolishly attacked King Agaja. Since we were no threat to the king, the dwarf must have told the tales for only one reason. He was sure that they would be passed on to the English in their big fort at the mouth of the river.

The last to be hauled aloft were Konje, my father and mother, Dondo, our servant, and me. The basket bumped against the stone sides of the dark hole. The rope creaked. Water dripped on us. The servants who were hauling us in sang. They stopped. The basket stopped. We dangled for a while, I think on purpose. My mother said that she wished she had stayed at home in our quiet village and I felt the same.

The dwarf had been left behind, I thought, but when the servants lifted us out of the basket, he was there, grinning. He pointed toward a flowery path lined with palm trees. At its end was a wall painted with the same color as the face of the cliff. Above the wall rose three broken turrets with the same zigzags and fish hooks in the Arabic language.

Speechless, every one of us save Konje overpowered by the dark hole dripping with water, the swinging basket, the tumbling walls and turrets that lay in front of us, we passed silently through an arch into a hall lit by torches.

The hall was hung with loops of colored cloth and there were cloth mats underfoot. The air, which smelled of frankincense, moved softly around us, stirred by a row of guards waving palm fronds.

3

From this hall we were herded into a courtyard that could easily hold a thousand guests. In its center were a pit and a pile of stones that once had been a fountain. Hooded vipers now sunned themselves among the stones.

Around the rim of the courtyard were small openings decorated with flowers. Here we were invited to refresh ourselves. Afterwards, the dwarf led us out of the courtyard through a dark passageway into an even larger courtyard, where the sky was hidden by strips of colored silk.

Smoke filled the air. Oxen and wildebeest turned on spits. Small boys caught the drippings and poured them on the turning meat. Plumed birds roasted on burning coals.

We ate sitting on the floor among flowerbeds. We sipped juices from big-eared jars. Horns and little tan-tan drums played music that none of us had ever heard before.

The dwarf waddled about, making sure that we

lacked nothing to eat or drink. But King Agaja did not appear. I began to think that he did not exist, that the dwarf himself was King Agaja. Then, with a blare of horns, painted warriors marched to the center of the courtyard.

On their shoulders was an ivory chair with gold ropes and bangles. In the chair, almost lost among the cushions, sat a man, no larger than the dwarf, draped in a yellow robe, with a red peaked hat on his head.

Horns and drums fell silent. Warriors that lined the walls of the courtyard touched their heads to the floor. A whispered word from Konje passed among us and we got to our knees, slowly, for none of us, being Christians, felt comfortable paying homage to a Muslim king.

The king spread his hands wide and spoke in a voice made bigger than he was, in the dialect of our village. He welcomed us to his kingdom. He held a cup to his lips and invited us to join him in an act of friendship.

Servants, while the king held the cup to his lips, poured cups of sparkling juice among us. The king drank and we drank. The king finished his cup and tossed it away. We finished our cups and we, too, tossed them away. The king laughed and we laughed.

Quickly, everything changed. The laughter ended. King Agaja, surrounded by his women guards, marched out of the courtyard, through an

11

arch of elephant tusks, into a room lit with hanging lamps. The dwarf motioned Konje and our Council of Elders to follow the king. A lattice door decorated with glittering gems closed behind them.

The women of our court and the women of King Agaja's court talked little to each other because we spoke different languages. I was uncomfortable.

Musicians played and sweets were served. Night came. The moon rose. Now and again voices sounded through the latticed door, but they were never clear enough for me to hear what was said. Still, I had the strong feeling that an argument had arisen between the king and our Council of Elders about something that could not be settled in a friendly way.

I was right, horribly right. Toward morning, when the moon was hidden by dark clouds, I was awakened by a hand clenched tight on my mouth, another hand at my throat, and a voice saying softly, "Quiet. You will not be harmed."

Sounds suddenly came from everywhere in the curtained room where our women were asleep. The sound of feet moving stealthily on the thick carpets, gasps, curses, a wild scream.

I was pulled to my feet and a length of silk scarf wound about my head. In the grasp of two men who lifted me in the air every few steps to hurry me along, I was taken to the cliff and sent down the yawning hole. There were seven people with me. Who they were, I didn't know until we reached the river and were lying in a war canoe.

In the first gray streaks of dawn I made out Konje, bound hand and foot, with something stuffed in his mouth and a gash on his cheek that hadn't stopped bleeding. Beside him was Dondo, also bound. In front of me was our slave Lenta and her two boys. It seemed to me that Agaja had picked out the six of us deliberately.

There were two canoes close behind us filled with people from our village. But I didn't see my family, my father and mother and my sister. I was never to see them again.

We went down the river fast, through the big loop the storm had made. As we passed our sleeping village, Konje tried to speak but only croaks came from his mouth. Dondo pointed toward the sea.

"Slave ships," he said. "They're waiting for us."

There were three of them where the river met the sea. Three ships that needed paint were anchored a good distance from each other. All had tattered flags flying from their masts.

As we passed the first of the ships, blacks called down to us. With raised fists they warned us of the evils to come. They told us to jump into the sea. Some told us to kill our captors before it was too late.

When we reached the third slave ship, we were

hauled on deck in a net. At the last minute, Konje struggled to get free. But he was still fastened to Dondo by chains. His struggles were ended when a smiling sailor gave him a blow on the head.

The ship had sailed north for many days before I saw Konje again. I worried about him, sure that his arrogance would get him in trouble. I grieved for him, fearing that he was dead. But the worry and the grief saved my life. It kept me from thinking about the terrible thing that had happened to me and my family. It kept me from slipping over the side of the ship some dark night when no one was looking, to my death.

When I caught sight of Konje again, he was no longer in chains. He was dressed in a red shirt and a yellow cap. He was the leader of a gang of slaves who washed the filth from the decks where we lived.

The ship was called *God's Adventure*. One of her owners was Len Sorensen. I had known Master Sorensen for five years. He had come to our village many times trying to buy slaves. He had bought none from Konje's father or from Konje, yet he was always friendly and brought us presents.

Three days later, when he saw me among the crowd of slaves he had gathered along the coast, he was also friendly. He didn't send me back to the village, but he found me a hole that was clean, where I could lie down and stand up. In the rest of the ship, the decks were so close together you had to lie flat on your back.

More helpful than this, he calmed some of my fears. I didn't believe that the white people where we were going were cannibals, as most of the others believed. They would work us hard but would not eat us.

The island of St. John, which was to be our home, was owned by Denmark, Master Sorensen told me. He said that it was far across the ocean, near America. He told me many things. He told me, for instance, how I would be sold to a white planter, how I should act.

"The planter who buys you," he said, "will put you to work in his household or in the sugar-cane fields. In the fields, under the hot sun, slaves don't last long, perhaps a year. So show your white teeth, Raisha, smile a lot, and don't say anything unless you're asked."

At first we talked in my dialect, but after a while Master Sorensen spoke in Danish and I learned some of his language. This was very helpful when I got to the island of St. John.

4

God's Adventure — such a hopeful name for a savage ship — took six months and more to sail from Africa to the islands. We left the mouth of the river in the night. We sailed slowly north along the slave coast and stopped at every port.

Captain Sorensen gathered in two or three slaves in each port. He was very particular. Ashantis he wouldn't buy because they caused trouble, he said. The Senegals were intelligent. The Congos were tall and beautiful. The Mandigos were lazy. The Ibos made good house servants, he told me, and bought ten of them.

God's Adventure was crowded before we ever left the village of Accra. The ship had four decks, piled one on top of the other, so close, as I have said, that you could not stand up. The new slaves choked the ship. Then a plague broke out and three or four of us died every day.

Lenta and her children lived on the lowest of the four decks. I never saw her until the plague began and I heard that her son, Madi, was sick. I carried him aloft to my place on the first deck. It turned out that he didn't have the plague. He just couldn't eat the fuzzy green meat and weevily mush he was given and threw them up.

I shared with him the food Captain Sorensen saw that I was given every day. Soon, as we turned back along the slave coast and picked up more slaves, Madi got well. His body was a bundle of bones, but he moved about, ate, and kept the food down.

Soon after we turned back a storm struck us. The ship with all her big cargo was top-heavy. She rolled like a log. Her bare masts dipped into the sea. She creaked and groaned. Gray waves rose up and engulfed the top deck, sweeping men into the sea.

The storm left us afloat off the port of Accra. Here Captain Sorensen took on more slaves to replace those he had lost from poor food, the plague, and the storm, and sailed westward toward the islands with three hundred eighty-one slaves.

We had not sailed far when the ship began to leak where her bottom timbers met the sea. The crack was small in width but long. Water poured in fast and began to flood the lower deck. Captain Sorensen sent sailors down to fix the leak, but they failed. If anything, the sea poured in faster.

He knew about Madi, knew that the boy had fingers like sticks and sent him down with a rope around his waist to poke strips of oiled cotton into the crack. After Madi worked for a while the sea-water came in more slowly.

They pulled him in, gave him a sip of rum, a bowl of corn and fresh meat, and sent him down again. His sticklike fingers worked cotton into the rest of the crack. The leak stopped.

It was dusk by now, and we were sailing along fast when they began to pull him in. One moment he was there, dangling with the rope around his waist, the next moment only half of him was there. Sharks had gotten the rest.

His death came close to bringing a revolt. We slaves talked of little else, until the sailors went around with whips, guards got out their muskets, and Captain Sorensen warned us that unless we quit talking he would give us water to drink but nothing to eat. He would also throw the leaders of any revolt into the sea.

The food got worse. The salted meat had green spots on it. The water in the mossy casks had things swimming around. And the ship stank. She was washed out every other day. Slaves were sent below to burn powder and kill the smells, but still the ship stank. Those in the two deepest decks began to die, three or four a day, and were thrown overboard. A school of gray sharks began to follow us.

Then everything changed. The food got better and there was more of it. One of the sailors told me that Master Sorensen was fattening us up.

"In less than two weeks," he said, "we will reach the islands. He wants everyone to look healthy."

I passed the news to the rest of the slaves, thinking that everyone would be happier, now that we were near the end of our journey. It had another effect. They had gotten used to their lives, bad as they were, and feared what would happen after they reached land.

All that Captain Sorensen had told me about the islands of St Thomas and St. John proved to be true. As we came into the harbor of St. Thomas and I saw the crowd in the streets, as many blacks as whites, gathered around the auction place, flags flying everywhere and bands playing, I remembered everything he had told me.

It seemed as if I had been there before. Even the slave pen with its rusty iron bars and swarms of black guards swinging whips I had seen many times.

Only when we were led onto a platform and I looked down into a ring of white faces sweating in the sun did I wonder if the other slaves were right after all. Perhaps these white men gazing up at me with their mouths half-open really were cannibals who ate people.

5

Captain Sorensen had decided to sell three of us together, Konje, Dondo, and me. Lenta looked grim and unhappy. She still grieved for her son, so she was kept to one side.

A man rapped his hammer on a stone. He was the auctioneer Captain Sorensen had told me about. "We have three prime slaves of the three hundred slaves *God's Adventure* brought to the island this day," he said. "Here is Konje, chief of the Barato tribe." He put a hand on Konje's shoulder. Konje flinched. "A great breeder of sons and daughters. A magnificent specimen."

Konje did look magnificent. They had covered him with palm oil. He was naked to the waist, and his muscles rippled in the broiling sun. He towered above the black guards standing against the wall and the man with the hammer.

The auctioneer said, pointing to me, "Raisha the daughter of a subchief. Comely, strong, mother of many strong, comely children. She also speaks the

Danish language. And Dondo, trained as a slave in a chieftain's family, is the perfect household servant."

He wiped his brow and banged his hammer. He banged it again until the crowd was quiet.

"These three, the finest Africa has to offer, will be sold as one," he said. "And no bid under two thousand rigsdalers will be considered. What do I hear?"

The auctioneer heard silence, then whispers among the planters. A man who stood just below me said to a woman wearing a pink dress and a flower in her hair, "What do you think, Jenna?"

"I think it's a bargain at three thousand rigsdalers," she said. "The man's worth that much alone."

"He's a little overpowering," the man said. "It would take a strong hand to control him."

"You have a strong hand, Jost."

Someone shouted an offer of two thousand four hundred rigsdalers. The auctioneer repeated the offer and gave the stone a blow.

"I like the girl, too," the woman said. "She has a nice smile."

It was the same smile I had learned on the ship, as if I had just received a gift I had always wanted. My face hurt from smiling and I felt like letting out a hair-raising scream. The deep blue eyes of Master Jost, blue as the sky, examined me from head to foot.

Offers were coming fast, a few rigsdalers at a time.

The woman said, "Don't be niggardly, Jost. We will be here all day. The sun is hot. Philippe Horn is over there writing on a piece of paper. He wants them badly. Get rid of him with an offer he cannot match."

Jost cleared his throat, cupped his hands, and shouted,"Three thousand rigsdalers."

The crowd fell silent. Men I took to be plantation owners, who stood down in front in big straw hats, looked at each other and shook their heads.

The auctioneer shouted, "Three thousand rigsdalers. Do I hear three thousand, one hundred?"

The silence grew. Master van Prok lifted his hat and put it on again. He seemed ready to make a higher bid.

"Three thousand," said the auctioneer, glancing down at the planters, calling each by name. "Gentlemen, what do I hear?"

He heard nothing. His hammer came down with a bang. "Sold, sold to Master van Prok of Hawks Nest for the sum of three thousand rigsdalers."

From the shadows a black man crept out and climbed the ladder to the platform where the three of us stood. He was tall but bent over by some misfortune, so that he shifted crablike from one side to the other as he moved along.

"Come," he said. "I will take you to the boat that

will take you to Hawks Nest on the island of St. John. St. John is only four miles away. It will be a pleasant voyage on this sunny day."

He took us past the pen that held the rest of the slaves that *God's Adventure* had brought to St. Thomas that day. Midnight black though they were, they looked like ghosts and were ghostly silent. My heart went out to them.

"What is your name?" Konje asked.

"Nero," the man said.

"What work do you do at Hawks Nest?"

"I am the bomba, Bomba Nero. I oversee what goes on at Hawks Nest. You can also call me Sir Bomba."

He talked out of the side of his mouth. His arrogance and cold, darting glance made Konje clamp his jaws.

At a shack by the wharf, the bomba took Konje inside. Two blacks put manacles on him. I saw them take a red-hot iron out of the fire and stamp a number on Konje's back. He made not a sound. They stamped Dondo, too.

We waited on the wharf for Jost van Prok and his wife. They came with two boys, good for running errands, Master van Prok told Nero when the bomba gave them a surly glance.

"I have two servants," Jenna van Prok said. "You will be my third. You will like that, I am sure."

"Oh, yes," I said.

23

It was the task I had worked for from the day Captain Sorensen had told me about it, that it was much better than working in the fields, out in sun and storm. It was why I had learned to be docile, to say nothing unless asked, and to smile even though it hurt.

St. John is a beautiful island, just a few miles from St. Thomas, across pale blue water. At dusk our small boat came to Hawks Nest, the van Prok plantation, and moored in the shallows. From here we all walked ashore, except Jenna van Prok.

She was carried to the beach on Konje's broad shoulders. As he bent to set her down on the sand, Bomba Nero glanced at him. It was a searching glance, little more than a lifting of an eyelid, but in it was hatred.

I told Jenna van Prok that Lenta, my friend, was a good cook and would be very helpful at the house.

"I bid for her," she said, "but the Haugaard brothers outbid me. They have a plantation close to Mary Point. It is near so you'll see her again."

She looked at me from under the rim of her pink hat. "You have a pretty smile, like an angel from heaven," she said. "I'm going to call you Angelica. Do you like that?"

"Yes," I said, though I didn't like the name at all.

The van Proks changed all our names. The mistress called Konje "Apollo." Her husband called

Dondo "Abraham." This was a custom, I learned. The planters wanted the slaves to forget they were born in Africa, that they were black Africans.

"Do you understand what I say?" Jenna van Prok asked. "The language I speak?"

"Yes, when you don't speak fast," I said.

6

Hawks Nest looked down upon the sea. It was neither small nor large among the plantations on the mountainous island of St. John, but half of its land was level, good for the growing of sugar cane.

The rest of the plantation was cut up by gullies, bushy ravines, and by rock-strewn peaks. Here Master van Prok had cleared the land and terraced it for the growing of cotton.

The van Prok house stood on a low cliff within sound of the sea. It was made of stone and timber and looked like a small fort.

The slave huts stood at a distance from the house beside a large pile of boulders, the men on one side, women on the other. In the middle of the boulders were privies. They were far enough from the house not to be unpleasant for the van Proks.

My hut, like all the others, had stone walls and a roof of palm leaves. One side was open and faced the sea. This was a help because sometimes in the night cool winds blew from that direction.

The first night I slept in my hut, I was told by the van Proks' slaves that for a year now, a terrible drought had settled upon the island. Great white clouds would come up at dawn, spread across the sky, and turn black, but not a drop of rain would fall.

This is exactly what happened on my first night. Dawn broke clear, with a small sea wind. The white clouds came up. The sun burned holes in them. They spread across the sky and turned black, but no rain fell. The clouds disappeared during the night. The heavens were on fire with stars.

Before I went to bed, Jenna van Prok had whispered to me, "My husband has told the bomba to put you to work in the fields tomorrow. This is his habit with all new slaves. He likes to test them. Don't despair. In a week I will have you working in the house."

A tutu horn blew just before dawn, a wild sound from a conch shell. Roosters crowed. The bomba came up the path, banging his ironwood club against everything in his way.

"Out!" he shouted. "This is not Sunday. It is a Wednesday in the month of April. You are not in Africa, dreaming about a breakfast of melons and roasted birds. You're on the plantation of Master van Prok, on the island of St. John in the Danish West Indies among the Virgin Islands. Out!"

We went to the side of a hill in a bushy ravine. There were fifteen of us, all but Konje, who was sent to work at the sugar mill. Before the drought, I was told, cotton grew in the ravine at this time of year and there would be pink flowers on the bushes. Now all was scorched and dry. With long knives we cut down the bushes and stirred up the ground.

In midmorning boys brought our breakfasts — a handful of dried finger-sized fish called poorjack and shriveled chickpeas, but nothing to drink. Already the sun beat down. It burned hotter than it ever did in Barato.

At noon we rested for a while. It was the time when the slaves went off to work in their little plots of land to raise vegetables for themselves. Now all they could do was to scratch at the scorched earth and pray on their knees for rain.

After the sun went down the bomba came and said that we hadn't done much that day, that we didn't deserve even the little fried fish his boys handed out to us.

After three days in the field I found that they ate better food at the van Proks'. Fearing that I would collapse from the work and the heat, Mistress Jenna had made her husband change his mind about testing me for a whole week.

She brought me into the house and I became her body servant, one of three, as she had said. With Amina, a slave she'd had for years, I attended her from dusk until midnight and ate my supper from what the van Proks left over.

We ate salt pork from Holland, salt mutton from

New England, and bread baked in St. Thomas. Sometimes the bread had weevils in it, which I picked out before Mistress Jenna was served.

The food was not good. Master van Prok complained about it. "They send us meat that the market has refused," he said. "Meat so tough it bends the teeth. And the salt! You have to drink a firkin of water to calm your thirst. And at this moment there's not that much water on the whole plantation."

For the slaves and the van Proks water to drink ran out after the second meal of the day, except for what was needed for the mules that turned the millstones that ground the cane for molasses and rum.

All three of Mistress Jenna's body servants were made to work in the distillery five hours each day. Master van Prok's three male servants hauled water up the hill for five hours, too. Among the three was Dondo. He had worked in the fields for days, until Mistress van Prok discovered that he was good at trimming hair. He then was brought into the household.

From the very beginning, Konje had hauled water up the hill from the sea. He could carry two times more water than any of the other slaves. More weight and much faster. He would put a cask on top of his head and go up the steep hill half running.

The bomba picked up Konje's new name, and

when I was working in the distillery I heard him call out, "Apollo, you're a wonder. I, too, was a wonder, like you, but see what the hammer did."

Then he grinned and beat the ground with his club. He was punishing Konje, little by little, to get rid of his arrogance.

One of the slaves told me that the bomba had once been a giant of a man. But he had run away and when he was caught, instead of cutting off one of his legs, as was the law, they broke his bones with a hammer. Then they put them together wrong. Strangely, after that he loved the white people and hated the slaves.

Konje knew what the bomba was trying to do, but when I told him that he was killing himself, he only clenched his hands.

7

Late one afternoon, when the distillery had been running on sugar cane stored months before, and Konje had hauled more seawater than ever, a ship sailed into Hawks Nest Bay. A cannon went off, horns sounded, and a flag ran up the mast.

The cannon shot roused Jost van Prok, who lay in his hammock asleep. I had just gone to work with his wife's hair, making the three little curls she wore on her forehead.

Master van Prok bounded to his feet and ran to the window that looked down on the bay.

"Spaniards," he shouted in his bull-like voice. "Devil's spawn. Robbers from Puerto Rico. What will they want for their water this time? Last year it was two rigsdalers a tubful. Twice that this time, you can be sure!"

Mistress Jenna skipped to the window. "What good fortune!" she cried. "No matter the cost. Now we can have a garden. Now we can fatten a few sheep and eat fresh meat instead of that salt stuff from Holland."

She was beside herself. The whole plantation was excited, for now every slave could plant a small garden. Everyone was excited except Jost van Prok, who had to pay.

The Spaniards sold the water at three rigsdalers a tubful. A tubful was what a slave could carry on his head. The tubs were all the same size. A small man could carry a tub a third full. A strong man a tub two-thirds full of water.

This was how Konje became the most important slave on Hawks Nest plantation. He could carry a full tub on his head, up the long hill path to the storehouse, without spilling a drop.

The Spanish captain was not pleased with Konje. And when Master van Prok cut the number of carriers to four, to Konje and three others, the captain threatened to sail away unless he was paid double the number of rigsdalers.

Master van Prok paid, muttering under his breath, "Thieves. Spanish cutthroats." But the water had brought the plantation to life. The storehouse rang with laughter. Slaves sang. They came down from the fields and worked.

Many of the rain barrels in the storehouse had dried out and fallen apart. They had to be put together again. Our two carpenters worked all day and by torchlight. Dozens of barrels still had water in them, but, full of wriggling eggs and young mosquitoes, they had to be cleaned out.

The bomba went around banging his ironwood club, with a smile for everyone except Konje.

It was dusk. Konje had been working since dawn. He came into the yard while I was bringing Mistress Jenna's supper from the cookhouse. His feet dragged and water spilled over the side of the barrel.

After he had emptied the barrel and come out of the storehouse, I made him sit down. I offered him a piece of Mistress Jenna's salt mutton. He refused it but took a drink from her cup of rum, then spat it out.

The bomba had been watching us from the shadows. He came limping across the yard and looked down at Konje sprawled on the ground.

"You are not to drink Mistress Jenna's rum," he said. "You are not to touch the cup she uses. Do you understand?"

Konje did not answer. It was an insult not to answer, but the bomba let it go when he saw Konje get to his feet.

We waited until he was in the house, probably telling the van Proks all that had happened.

"I have noticed the distillery is at work," Konje said. "There's fire under all the pots. One of the pots is full of muscovado."

Muscovado was the coarse yellow sugar left in the first pot as the sugar cane started down the line.

"When I quit tonight, after one more barrel, I'll introduce the bomba to the muscovado. They'll make a good mixture, don't you think?"

"You can't do that. They'll cut you up into small pieces. Besides, Nero is a sick man. You can take his insults, we both can."

"For how long?"

"Until we find some way to escape."

"I've found a way already. I was told by sailors on the Spanish ship that there are runaways at Mary Point. They don't know how many. They think ten or twelve. Mary Point is surrounded on three sides, they say, by straight up-and-down cliffs. On the fourth side is a cactus wall so thick that a snake can hardly get through it."

"How are you to get through?"

"I'll find a way. The way the runaways found."

"What will I do?"

"You'll stay here until I come for you."

"In a year?"

"Before then."

"I'll die."

"You will not die. You will live and I will come for you."

"When are you going?"

"Tonight."

He lifted me off the ground and kissed me. He put the empty barrel on his head and started down the trail. I listened until I could hear his footsteps no more.

8

At the moment when the big drum at Mary Point began to talk, the sand in the sand clock quietly ran out. I turned the clock upside down and started the sand flowing again. Jost van Prok was very particular about the hours between dusk and dawn, for these were the hours of terror.

Now that three months had gone by, the talk came from the west and from the east, from everywhere the runaway slaves had a camp. The talk was the same as last night and the night before and many nights before that. The big drum at Mary Point always talked the loudest. It was the drum Jost van Prok feared the most.

After I turned the sand clock, I went to comfort Mistress Jenna. The sand flies were bad. They're tiny, you can scarcely see them, but they have a ferocious bite. Mosquitoes were bad, too, though for months now not a drop of rain had fallen. Most of my twelve hours as her body slave were spent waving a palm leaf fan.

Master van Prok lay in his hammock, with his legs hanging over the sides, rocking himself to sleep after a small supper of needlefish and yams. At the sound of the drums he put his feet on the floor and sat bolt upright. He was a stout man, as thick through as he was wide, with long arms and knotty fists. He stared through the doorway into the night with his cold blue eyes. His whip lay coiled beneath the hammock.

"The runaways are making a good time of it," Mistress Jenna said. "But once their food disappears, they'll come running back."

"*Ours* will disappear first," Master van Prok said. "They steal from the storehouse. They steal from the fields. And our slaves give them food on the sly."

"You worry so about the runaways," his wife said. "Why is it that you and our neighbors don't arm yourselves and wipe them out?"

"Because it would take ten times the number we could muster," Jost van Prok said. "The runaways would never stand and fight. They'd slink off somewhere and we would never find them again. These new slaves, the bussals, are different from the slaves who were born in the islands. If we did capture these new ones, they would up and kill themselves. To die by his own hand means to a bussal that his spirit returns to Africa and lives once more in the bodies of a nobleman. Or so I am told."

"How silly," Mistress Jenna said.

"The only way to control the runaways is by stricter laws. We've been far too gentle with them," Jost van Prok said.

Dondo stood beside the hammock, waving a fan. At the words, "too gentle," the fan hung still in the stifling air.

Master van Prok pointed a finger at Dondo. "What do the drums say?" he asked.

"I do not understand the drums," Dondo answered.

"Angelica," Master van Prok said, pointing the finger at me, "you've been here for months. You have heard the drums talk. What do they say?"

I knew the drum talk. I knew what the drums were saying. The runaways planned a revolt against all of the white plantations on the island of St. John. They were getting ready, storing guns and knives and food. It would take months. It would be November before they were ready to revolt.

"What do the drums say?" the master asked again, still pointing his finger at me.

"I do not know about the drums, sir."

"You should know, especially about the big one at Mary Point. The man you think about night and day, Apollo, the one you are thinking about now, while you stand there looking so innocent. He is the one who tells the big drum what to say."

Mistress Jenna stopped sipping the air I stirred up with my palm leaf fan. "Forget about the drums," she said to her husband. "Why not ask

Governor Gardelin to bring his army and have a wonderful parade? A parade will impress the new slaves and the old slaves, too."

"An army? The governor doesn't have an army," her husband replied.

The cat was after the house gecko, stalking the shiny lizard along the shelf that ran around the room. I was told to put the cat outside. By the time I caught him, my tasks were nearly done for the day.

I helped Mistress Jenna get into her nightdress and brought her a cup of Kill Devil rum. Kill Devil came out of the coils first, raw and strong enough to kill the devil himself. Before the drums began to talk so much, she drank Kjeltum, the rum that came out last and was much milder.

She drank the Kill Devil from a small cup with cupids painted around the rim. She drank two of these cups of rum. Then she looked around in her closet and found a dress she hadn't worn for a long time. She told me to put it on. The dress was far too large, but I put it on over my cotton shift.

Master van Prok raised up from his hammock and said that I was prettier in my shift, without the dress. This did not please Mistress Jenna.

9

I would not see Konje tonight. Since dusk as I waited on Mistress Jenna I had said this to myself. I said it to myself as I walked up the path to my hut. I had seen him four nights ago.

It was a dangerous walk from the camp at Mary Point, through steep ravines and rock-strewn gullies, four long miles back and forth, at night. It could be weeks before he came again. It was better to know this than to look for him in vain.

A half moon shone in the west. I passed the mimosa tree where I always met him. I did not look.

Drums were talking. Waves broke on the rocks below. Voices drifted down from the slave huts. Yet suddenly I heard soft steps in the dust. It could be a spirit following me. I did not turn around and walked faster.

The night wind was behind me. On it I heard my name called, called twice before I could stop.

He was there, tall and shining in the moonlight under the mimosa tree. My heart was a bird. It beat against my breast.

"You went by haughty," he said, "and did not even look."

"I was afraid to look for fear you were not there," I told him, quickly, in what little voice I had.

He felt the sleeve of my dress. "I was afraid to speak to you when you went by. I didn't know you in a dress. I thought you were somebody else. Where did it come from?"

"From Jenna Prok. She gave it to me."

"Another gift."

He took out a necklace of blue stones, the kind the sea polishes and leaves on the beach, and put it over my head and around my neck. He lifted me high. He enclosed me like a storm cloud.

When he set me down, I said, "You promised to take me with you the next time you came."

"Food's scarce at the camp," he said. "We have more people than we can feed. In another month it will be different. I will come for you then."

"That is a long time off," I said.

"It may be sooner," Konje said. "We heard from St. Thomas this morning that the governor is on his way to Hawks Nest. He'll be here tomorrow and stay for a few days, talking to planters, spying on things. He'll bring powder and bullets from the fort, like the last time. Tell Dondo that we need

41

both. Tell him to steal what he can. Tell Dondo to hide them here behind me in the cactus."

"I will tell him tomorrow morning," I said, "when he is through with Master van Prok."

The drums at Mary Point had stopped talking. No waves broke on the shore below. In the silence there was a sound I often had heard.

It was Master van Prok and his whip, the tschickefell. He was walking up the path that led to the huts. He did this every night, now that runaways were camped at Mary Point. He wanted to scare any of his slaves who might be tempted to join them.

The whip was long, woven of strips of goatskin, and had a piece of metal at its tip. From twenty feet away he could flick a bird from a branch. The tschickefell cracked like a pistol shot.

The sounds came closer. Konje lifted me again and set me down. "Tell Dondo," he whispered. "Do not forget." Quickly, he was gone.

I went to my hut and took off the dress and stretched out on my mat. Master van Prok circled the huts, cracking his whip.

Before dawn, at four o'clock when the field slaves went to work, I hid the necklace under my mat. I put on the dress and went down to the house to give Dondo Konje's message, afraid I might miss him.

The van Prok toilet was outside the house. The

sun rose over the ridge and Master van Prok came out naked and stretched himself. After he was through with the toilet, he bent over and Dondo whisked him clean with a horsetail brush. This was the custom of the planters on the island of St. John and the island of St. Thomas. They would not think of starting the day otherwise. Dondo did this task with his jaws set tight.

I waited until Master van Prok had gone down to the distillery, where the mules were going around, turning the grinding stones that crushed the sugar cane. Then I gave Dondo the message Konje had given me.

He shook his head. "I stole powder when Governor Gardelin was here two months ago. Remember?"

"I remember. You almost got caught."

"Almost. I had a bagful, all I could carry. I hid in the cave under the hill. The guards searched the house. They searched the beach. They were about to search the cave when the tide came in. The tide kept them out but it soaked the powder. Since that time van Prok hides it in a closet near his hammock. Sometimes, when he's asleep, when I am waving the fan, I have had a notion to put some fire in the closet."

The way Dondo spoke, this was more than a notion with him. "You'll blow yourself up," I told him. "Me, too."

"I will do it when you're not around."

"Thank you," I said.

"I will get Konje some powder."

"He wants you to be careful."

"I'll get powder," Dondo said. "And be careful."

10

While we were talking, Governor Gardelin's ship was seen on the blue waters between the island of St. Thomas and the island of St. John. Master van Prok left the sugar mill and hurried to the fort. It was a thatched hut, a stone wall, a stone platform, and a cannon. The cannon puffed quietly. It was answered by three loud roars from the ship.

"Big roars," Dondo said, "mean the governor has a lot of powder and he's angry."

"The governor's always angry," I said.

The ship sailed into the bay and the anchor went down and two men were rowed in close to the beach. Mistress Jenna named them. One, Governor Gardelin, came the rest of the way on a slave's shoulders. The other was Preacher Isaak Gronnewold, she said. He refused to be carried on the backs of black men. Instead, he stepped into the water and got his pants wet.

A longboat left the ship and landed on the beach.

It was piled high with food, which the slaves balanced on their heads and carried up the trail to the cookhouse.

They carried thick-leafed kaleloo, bunches of ellube herbs to sprinkle around, Guinea corn and okra, sweet-rooted taro, sugar apples, a basket of fish — not pot fish or salted poorjack but big fish from deep water, red meat — bundles of it, and firkins of beer.

Last came three sacks marked with X's. They were heavy. The slaves who carried them panted under the weight.

"Powder," Dondo whispered.

We watched them carry the food into the cookshed and the three sacks of powder into the house.

"They will put it in the closet," Dondo said, "near van Prok's hammock."

"Be careful," I warned him.

Laughter came from the house, but there was no laughter when I went in early to help Mistress Jenna. The door that faced the sea was open and the two men sat in the doorway, where what little breeze there was would reach them.

Philip Gardelin's pants were pulled up to air his naked knees. He was governor of the West India and Guinea company, king of everything they did or thought of doing. He frightened me. I was scared to be in the same house with him.

The governor was talking to Isaak Gronnewold,

the minister on St. John, a tall young man burned almost black by the sun.

"I see you brought your Bible, though it's against the law," the governor said. "You carry it around and preach it to the slaves, and I permit you to do so. But it hasn't made any difference that I can see. They're a benighted lot."

"I have been preaching the Bible for only two years," the minister said. "Others have preached for hundreds of years. And most of us, all of us, are still benighted."

"Why do we have so much sickness on St. John?" the governor asked. "On St. Thomas there's nothing like this. If it goes on, we won't have a slave left."

"And it will go on," Minister Gronnewold said, "until the slaves are given food fit to eat. You will notice that not one of the planters has died from starvation."

Master van Prok's tschickefell lay under his chair. He picked it up and laid it in his lap. "My slaves eat as well as I do. Am I to blame for the drought and the hurricanes that have ruined their gardens? Is it my fault that the slaves have forgotten what work is, if they ever knew? And how do I keep them from running away when the bush is filled with runaways and the nights with talking drums?"

As the governor started to answer the questions, Mistress Jenna called me away to help with her bath. She could have gone down to the sea and bathed, but she didn't like the salt the seawater left on her skin. She bathed in the seawater hauled up the hill when the salt was boiled out.

After I bathed and dressed her, she joined the men. The talk changed.

Nothing more was said about sickness and starvation and death. Governor Gardelin did the talking. It was about the happy life in Denmark, how he hoped to bring the same happiness to the Virgin Islands someday.

Mistress Jenna smiled at these words and drank another cup of Kill Devil. Every day now she drank more of this heavy rum.

11

The sun stood overhead when six men and their body servants rode in from plantations close by. It was a very hot day. A firkin of beer was carried in and everybody drank to Governor Gardelin, then to themselves.

Wonderful smells came from the cookhouse. I helped to put the daytime meal on the table. Everybody was too hungry to listen much to the governor, who went on talking about the happy days in Denmark.

Before the meal was over, Master van Prok sent Dondo out with a message for the field slaves. They had started work at four o'clock in the morning and had not eaten yet. The message invited them to the cookhouse, where a pig was roasting.

The slaves came trooping down in a happy mood. They gathered around the fires and were given slices of the roasted pig. Then they were told to go to their huts and sleep for the rest of the afternoon. They thanked the governor and went off singing.

At dusk Master van Prok called them down to the cookhouse again. They gathered around as they had before, looking for more of the roasted pig. There were nine women, nine children, and twelve men. Three of the men had run away.

The planters came out of the house and sat on the stone wall in front of the cookhouse with their servants behind them. Carrying his Bible, Isaak Gronnewold came out, then Governor Gardelin and Master van Prok. Mistress Jenna, who had drunk two cups of Kill Devil rum, fell asleep in her chair.

Now it was night. Slaves with torchwood flares stood on each side of the governor. He had a sheaf of papers in his hand.

"Apollo, who ran away from this plantation, is causing trouble at Mary Point," Governor Gardelin said. "He plans to revolt against all the plantations on St. John. To send him a warning, and to solemnly warn all slaves who may be tempted to follow him, I have written a new set of laws. The old laws for civil behavior, I have made stronger."

The night was stifling hot. Not a wisp of air came down from the hills or rose from the sea. Governor Gardelin paused for a drink of beer. His body servant handed him the sheaf of papers and the torchbearers moved closer to him so he could see.

"The leader of runaway slaves," he read from

the paper, "shall be pinched three times with red-hot irons, then hanged.

"Each runaway slave shall lose one leg, or, if the owner pardon him, shall lose one ear and receive one hundred and fifty stripes."

Isaak Gronnewold broke in upon him. "If these laws are held to, then the island of St. John will be the home of cripples, the dying, and the dead."

The governor held up a hand for quiet and went on. "Any slaves being aware of the intention of others to run away, and not giving information, shall be burned on the forehead and receive one hundred and fifty stripes.

"Those who inform of plots to run away shall receive ten dollars for each slave engaged therein.

"A slave who runs away for eight days shall have one hundred and fifty stripes; twelve weeks, shall lose a leg; and six months, shall forfeit his life, unless the owner pardon him with the loss of one leg."

These five laws were new. No one gathered there on that awful night had heard them before.

In the deep silence, even the children were quiet. Iron pinchers that glowed red hot we were used to. Master van Prok had a pair that hung in the sugar mill for all to see. There was also the whip that he carried everywhere. One hundred and fifty lashes would strip the strongest man of his flesh and his life.

"Slaves who steal to the value of four dollars,"

the governor said, "shall be pinched and hanged; less than four dollars, to be branded, and receive one hundred and fifty stripes.

"Slaves who receive stolen goods, as such, or protect runaways, shall be branded, and receive one hundred and fifty stripes.

"A slave who lifts his hand to strike a white person, or threatens him with violence, shall be pinched and hanged, should the white person demand it; if not, to lose his right hand."

Governor Gardelin paused again to sip his beer. The planters spoke in low voices and passed around a mug of Kjeltum rum.

"One white person shall be sufficient witness against a slave; and if a slave be suspected of crime, he can be tried by torture."

A woman began to cry. Torture was something new on the island of St. John.

The drums on the near side of Hawks Nest Hill began to talk. They talked with two words, Torture and Death. The words were picked up at once by drums on the far side of the hill and by drums to the north and west.

The governor paused at the sounds. He took another sip of beer and wiped his mustache with his hand.

"No slaves will be permitted to come to town with clubs or knives, or fight with each other, under penalty of fifty stripes.

"Witchcraft shall be punished with flogging.

"A slave who shall attempt to poison his master shall be pinched three times with red-hot iron, and then be broken on a wheel."

The drum beyond Hawks Nest Hill said, "Torture. Death." Then Konje's big drum at Mary Point spoke the words over and over, "Torture, Death, Torture, Death . . ." The drums filled the night.

"A free negro who shall harbor a slave or thief shall lose his liberty, or be banished," the governor said.

"All dances, feasts, and plays are forbidden unless permission be obtained from the master or overseer.

"Slaves shall not sell provisions of any kind without permission from their overseers.

"No estate slave shall be in town after drumbeat; otherwise he shall be put in the fort and flogged.

"The King's Advocate is ordered to see these regulations carried into effect.

"And I, Philip Gardelin, the King's Advocate, will see that they are carefully carried out, so help me God!"

He handed the papers to his body servant. He took his sword from its sheath and held it above his head. His sword glinted in the light of the torchwood flares.

12

Master van Prok was happy with the new laws. As soon as the governor put away his glittering sword, he clasped him around the shoulders, so excited he could hardly speak.

"Your laws are what we have prayed for," he said. "Many prayers are answered. Praise you, Governor Gardelin."

Master Duurloo, who owned a large plantation nearby, shouted, "Good work, Governor!"

But a planter from Cruz Bay was worried. "What happens," he said, "if one of my slaves is punished and can't work? I am not a big planter. I have only seven slaves. It would be a hardship to lose even one."

"Don't be disturbed," Governor Gardelin said. "My company will pay you the full worth of a slave if he's crippled, or, if you wish, replace him with a healthy slave."

"One good slave for a crippled slave?"

"Exactly."

"When?"

"As soon as a slave ship comes in."

"What if a ship does not come in?"

"You'll wait until a ship does come in," the governor said. He was getting impatient with the planter from Cruz Bay. "Would you like to go along the old way? Slaves disappearing into the bush one by one?"

"Oh, no."

"A hundred runaways gathered at Mary Point, ready at any moment to swoop down upon us and cut our throats?"

"God forbid!"

There were no more questions from the planters. They trooped into the house, drank the rest of the beer, and fell asleep on the porch. Minister Gronnewold hung his hammock under a tree. Governor Gardelin took his soldiers back to the ship, where he felt safer.

Without a sound, like so many naked ghosts, the slaves trudged silently to their huts. But at midnight, when I had given Mistress Jenna her last drink of Kill Devil for the day and settled her in bed, I found them whispering beside a small fire among the rocks.

All the slaves were there except Felicity. She was an accustomed slave — that's someone born in slavery and knowing nothing else. She was a pretty woman, twenty years old, and had four children. She would never think of running away.

The other slaves didn't like her. Truthfully, they didn't like me, either. They were suspicious of me because I was a body servant and worked in the house, not with them in the fields. Not one of the slaves was loyal to the van Proks. They stopped whispering when I came up, so I said good night and went to my hut.

Master van Prok wandered up the path with his whip. He had drunk too much and the whip didn't crack as it usually did. Still, the slaves heard it. When he went past they were silent.

He paused and called my name. "Are you asleep in there?"

I did not answer.

He thrust his head under the crossed branches that held up the roof. "Angelica, do you hear me?" He said this with a slur. He had swallowed a lot of rum and beer. If I was asleep, he would wake me up. I sat up and said, "I hear you, Master van Prok."

"Good. I want you to know that Governor Gardelin's new laws don't mean you. They are meant only for the thankless, the senseless, the scum who have forgotten how fortunate they are. Do you understand?"

"Yes," I said, crossing my middle fingers so as to turn the word *Yes* into a lie.

"It's been a hard year for us. The hurricane that leveled our fields, the terrible drought, which still holds us in its grip. Poor crops of sugar cane and therefore little rum, our livelihood. Now the runaways and the awful threat of a revolt. You can see how we are pressed against a stone wall."

I did see. For a moment I even felt sorry for Master van Prok and his troubles. For all the planters on all the islands.

"You have read Gronnewold's Bible," he said. "You know that the law of an eye for an eye, a tooth for a tooth was the rule in ancient times. It was successful then and it will be successful now."

Never before had he talked to me in this way.

"We have tried everything else and failed," he said.

I felt bolder than I had ever felt since the day I stood in the slave pen. "You have tried everything except freedom," I said.

His shoulders stiffened. He cleared his throat.

"Freedom will come," he said.

"When, sir?"

"When the slaves are ready."

"They are ready now. They have had enough of the hot pinchers and whips and the hammers that crush bones."

He stepped inside the hut and stood over me. "Freedom," he said. "They do not know what freedom means. Do you?"

"In Africa I was free."

"To do what? Sleep in the sun? Eat monkey meat and dance?"

The big drum was talking again. "Boom de, Boom de, Boom."

Master van Prok flung out his arms and began to dance to the sound of the big drum. Then he said, "Sleep, eat, dance. That's all you know about freedom, like the rest of the slaves, those who have sawdust in their heads instead of brains."

Out of breath, he stopped dancing and stood over me again. "You know what?" he said in a hoarse voice. "I am going to set you free. Tomorrow I will sign papers and send them to the office in St. Thomas. But you are free now, right now, at this moment."

I lay stiff with fear.

He leaned over me. His shadow filled the hut. "You are free, I tell you. Why do you not rise up and dance with joy?"

I did not move.

"Dance!" He shouted.

I could not move.

I shouted back at him. "Free the slaves on this plantation, then I will dance."

He gasped. "God in heaven! Free the slaves? You wish to ruin me?"

"Free them," I said quietly.

"Not one. And not you either. My mind has

changed. You are still a slave and always will be."

He backed away and cleared his throat. "I've had too much to drink."

He stumbled out of the hut. I heard him stagger down the trail, cracking the tschickefell.

13

Master van Prok and his tschickefell were still moving down the path when Dondo came. He sat down and pulled a thorn from his bare foot.

"When Prok left the house I got into the powder," he said. "I took enough powder for eighteen or twenty pistol shots. I hid it where you told me to, beyond the mimosa tree, in the cactus. I wrapped it up. If it rains it won't wash away. Not tomorrow, but soon, I will take more. But that's the end. I am afraid to take more."

I lay awake after he was gone. The big drum at Mary Point was talking, seven notes over and over, ten times, then a pause. It was counting the time before the day of the revolt. All the slaves from Mary Point to Coral Bay were listening. Across the bay on St. Thomas Island the slaves would be listening, too.

Before dawn a north wind sprang up. The sky clouded over and rain began to fall. I hurried down the trail to the cactus bush to see if the powder was dry. It was gone. I searched carefully. The powder was gone. Konje had been there.

I felt angry that he hadn't bothered to tell me. Then I felt ashamed of myself. He was always in danger when he traveled from Mary Point to Hawks Nest.

The rain drifted off and the sky cleared, but the wind still blew. A short distance from our shore lay Whistling Cay, a tumbled pile of rocks and caves with a coral reef surrounding them.

If a north wind blew, strange noises came from the cay. Sometimes they sounded like a child. Sometimes like the cries of a wounded beast, a serpent from the deeps. Other times the sounds were like the cooing of doves. On this night, while Konje was on his way back to Mary Point, the sounds were like his footsteps in the dust.

The sky clouded over yet again. A breath of rain sizzled in the dust. Nero the bomba blew the tutu. The horn roused the big red rooster. He stretched his neck and helped to rouse the field slaves. In the black dark before dawn they went to work building a terrace on the hill behind the mill for the cotton roots Master van Prok hoped to plant.

Usually, I slept beyond the bomba call. But sooner than an hour, with the first light, Isaak Gronnewold would be up. This was the time we talked together when he came to Hawks Nest.

I hurried down the cliff to the beach and took my bath. The water was clear as air. I waded out shoulder deep, then swam back to the shore and put on the dress Mistress Jenna had given me.

I watched Preacher Gronnewold walk down the trail. I thought he would never reach the shore. He would take a step or two, then stop and read his Bible, then look at the sky and the sea, then take another step or two.

"Good morning," I shouted when he was only halfway down the trail. He didn't answer, but after that he closed the Bible and came fast. He had long thin legs like a stork. They straddled the rocks, leaped the bushes.

I met him at the bottom of the trail and fell to my knees, for Isaak Gronnewold loved all the slaves on the island of St. John, even the runaways, even black-browed Nero. It was strange to me that he could love everyone, good or bad, yet he did, he did.

Isaak Gronnewold put out a long, bony hand and got me to my feet. He didn't like my bows, what he called "prostrations," yet I made them anyway, I had to.

"Last night," he said, "you heard Governor Gardelin set down new laws?"

"I heard."

"The other slaves heard?"

"They heard."

"But do you believe, do the other slaves believe,

that the new laws are only threats to scare the timid, to warn the bold?"

"I don't know what the others believe. I believe that the governor is a cruel man. He is pleased to have an excuse to be cruel. The laws were cruel enough before he changed them."

"The new laws are not threats. They are real. You and all of Master van Prok's slaves must understand this."

"They understand. I understand."

"Before the new laws, when we had the old laws, I went from plantation to plantation. And I read from the Bible many Sundays during the last year."

"Yes, you read over and over, 'What doth the Lord require of thee but to walk humbly with thy God?'"

"That was not done. Slaves from Cruz Bay to Hawks Nest and from here to Mary Point and from there to Coral Bay and back did not walk humbly. Instead, many ran away and hid in the bushes. Now there are runaways scattered all over the island, three hundred of them. More than three hundred. And more flee every day."

"You read other things from the Bible, too. You read what Christ told his friends when he went into the mountain. He told them, 'Blessed are the meek, for they shall inherit the earth.' He said other things, but these are the words that you said every time you talked to us. You said them at every plantation on the island. 'Blessed are the meek, for they shall inherit the earth.' I remember that I didn't know what 'inherit' meant and you said, 'It means "own." ' The meek shall own the earth."

Minister Gronnewold pulled at his nose. "I remember," he said, as if he did not wish to remember.

"Is that what you are going to say to us now? Do you want us to obey the new laws?"

"The new laws are bad. So bad they will destroy themselves, one by one."

"But until that time, until they do destroy themselves, we should obey them?"

"You *must* obey them. There's no other choice."

"We can run away. Dozens have. Over two hundred are hiding at Mary Point right now."

"Yes, but they starve."

"Better to starve. . ."

Cannon shot rang out from Governor Gardelin's ship. It lay anchored far out in the bay, too far to be surprised by enemies. Puffs of dirty white smoke drifted up and floated toward us. A yellow flag fluttered in the wind. The deck swarmed with guards in bright red uniforms.

"That is true, dear Raisha." He and Konje were the only ones who ever called me by my true name. "It shall come to pass."

"When?"

He looked away, far out into the distance.

"When?" I asked again. "When will the meek inherit the earth?"

64

He shook his head. "It has been many years since Christ spoke these words. And it may be many more."

"While we're alive?"

"Alas, no. But never unless we are meek."

"I understand," I said, though I did not.

14

Cannon roared. Puffs of smoke floated up again. Governor Gardelin came down the ship's ladder. He scrambled into a boat draped with flags and was rowed toward shore. In the shallows he climbed on the shoulders of two guards. But after a few steps, as one of the guards stumbled, the governor fell into the water.

He came up shouting, waving his arms, and was rowed back to his ship. I didn't see him until nearly noon. They had a horse for him now. He came up from the beach surrounded by guards, with two musicians playing. Slaves were called from the fields to stand and bow. I was invited to join them. He talked to Isaak Gronnewold, who was going to Mary Point to talk to the runaways.

The governor gave him a paper with his new laws written on it. "Read to them," he said.

"They know about the laws already," Preacher Gronnewold said. "The drums have told them."

"Be sure to tell them again," the governor said.

"I will gladly do so, sir."

"And tell Konje that if he sends his runaways back to the plantations they have foolishly fled, I will forgive them despite the law. None will be punished except for two bites each from the tongs and ten stripes. They will lose no legs or arms or their lives."

"Yes, sir." Isaak Gronnewold said.

He put the paper between the leaves of the Bible and tied it on his donkey's back. The Bible had a wood and goatskin cover. The wood was splintered and the long goat hair was worn off. He got on his donkey and started up the trail for Mary Point. I ran along beside him.

"Please give all my love to Konje," I said.

"I will do so."

"But save some for yourself."

"I will."

He stopped when we reached the gully that swooped down, then up again. He was riding a gray donkey. He liked donkeys better than horses because he liked to swing his long legs and touch the earth.

"Shall I tell Konje to come back?" he asked me.

"Konje will not come back, whatever I say."

"Do you want him to come back?"

"No. I will be with him when there's enough food at Mary Point."

Isaak Gronnewold reached out with a bony hand and grasped my shoulder. "Listen," he said, "there will never be enough food at Mary Point. The runaways only get what they steal and what the slaves give them. That will end with the new laws and the guards that will scour every hill and valley on the island, starting this very day."

I wanted to be angry with him but, though I stopped breathing at the awful thought, I knew that he spoke the truth.

As if he were a prophet speaking from the Bible, he said, "Unless Konje and his runaways give up, they shall be slain, man, woman, girl, and boy."

"Perhaps the Lord will think of a miracle, like the miracle when he parted the sea in the middle and walls of water were on both sides of the children of Israel and they went through on dry land and were saved from the Egyptians."

"The children of Israel slaved in Egypt for four hundred and thirty years before they were saved. The slaves of St. John have slaved on this island for scarcely ten years."

"Do we have to slave hundreds of years before the sea parts in the middle and we can go free?"

"I pray day and night that the sea will part much sooner. You must pray too, and ask the others to pray."

"I do pray. All the slaves pray."

"The Lord will hear us," said Isaak Gronnewold.

We came to the bottom of the gully. There was a hollow place to one side of the trail where a pool

68

of water had collected. Grass had started to grow around the edges. The donkey veered from the trail and began to graze.

Preacher Gronnewold pulled on the halter, but the donkey went on eating. He spoke to it, saying gentle words from the Bible. He sometimes spoke to the birds and animals as if they were people.

The beast went on cropping the grass. Preacher Gronnewold explained that they had miles to go and work to do. The beast pricked up its ears and listened but went on eating. I also had work to do.

"My friend," Preacher Gronnewold said to the donkey, "if you move on, I'll read from Exodus, your favorite part of the Bible. You can eat the rest of the grass when we return."

I searched around, as he kept up this conversation, and found a branch from a dead tree. With it I gave the beast a good whack, which sent them on their way.

"Give my love to Konje," I shouted again.

He didn't answer, but raised the Bible and waved. His legs were flying. It looked like a six-legged donkey plunging up the trail.

When I got back, running because I was late, Governor Gardelin and his red-coated guards, nearly fifty of them, were in front of the mill. He was telling the guards what he wanted that day. They were to divide into four squads, one squad going to the north, one to the south, one to the east, and one to the west.

"Stay on the regular trails, do not wander," he said. "Visit every plantation. I am giving the officer of each squad a list of my laws. Plantation owners will gather their slaves. The officer is to read to them every one of the new laws, slighting none."

The noonday sun seemed not to move in the sky. Drops of sweat formed on the governor's forehead. He stopped to rub them off.

"You are not to use your guns," he went on, "unless you are attacked, which is not likely. And you're to return to this plantation not later than Wednesday morning, this being Monday."

The guards rode off on their fine horses, straight in the saddle, laughing among themselves. They were happy, it seemed, to be leaving Governor Gardelin.

15

After I bathed Mistress Jenna, I brought her breakfast in from the cookhouse and food for Master van Prok's and Governor Gardelin's noonday meal. The governor had six guards standing watch outside the house. He worked on a paper as Dondo fanned him and swatted sand flies. Then he went back to his ship.

Master van Prok worked outside in the hot sun. He called the slaves down from the fields and had them gather bundles of pinguin. Pinguin has hundreds of crooked thorns that don't stick like cactus but tear your flesh. The slaves made pinguin ropes and tied them over the six windows of the house.

"Nobody will suddenly crash through a window," Master van Prok said to his wife, when he came in at dusk.

"Can't the pinguin be cut with sharp knives?" Mistress Jenna asked.

"Yes, but that takes time. It gives us a chance. We won't be surprised. We won't look up to see someone standing over us with a cane knife."

I was fanning the hot air, keeping the midges away from Mistress Jenna. At these words, a shudder ran through her body.

"I'm scared," she said.

She had been scared for weeks now. Master van Prok had heard these words many times. She was drinking a little more every day, which he did not like.

"You should go to St. Thomas," he said. "It's much safer in St. Thomas. They've had less than a dozen runaways and all have been caught and punished. You can leave with the governor when he leaves in a day or two."

She turned to me. "What do you think, Angelica?"

It was not an easy question to answer. I knew that she was in danger. All the white people were in danger. The danger grew more and more every day. I hunched my shoulders and said nothing.

"Speak up!" Master van Prok said.

"I don't know about the danger."

"You must know something."

At that moment, as the dusk deepened, the big drum at Mary Point began to talk. Another, a

72

smaller drum, south toward Cruz Bay, broke in.

"You know the drum talk, Angelica. What are they saying?"

"The small drum says that soldiers on horses have come and gone."

"The big drum says what?"

"It's jabbering."

"Jabbering about what?"

"Nonsense."

"What kind of nonsense?"

"It's just making a noise."

This was the truth but Master van Prok got up from his hammock and paced the floor. His heavy boots on the stones drowned out the sound of the drums.

He quit pacing. "Noise. Nonsense. Huh! You're the one making a noise. You're the one talking nonsense."

He pointed a finger at me. "You're lying, Angelica. Stop the fanning."

I put the fan aside.

"Look at me," he said.

I had never looked at Master van Prok, not since the first day on the plantation when he had reached out and touched my skin. I was angry then. I had looked him straight in the eye. He slapped me and said that I was not to look at him or at his wife or at any white person. I was to look up or down or to one side, but never straight into a white person's eyes. That was the custom on the island of St. John and the island of St. Thomas. If I ever did, I would be pinched with red-hot tongs.

Now that I had stopped fanning Mistress Jenna, she complained of the flies and the heat. Master van Prok asked her to be quiet.

"Angelica, look at me," he said.

I tried to look at him. But my eyes shifted about the room, at Dondo, at the house lizard stalking a fly, at Master van Prok's ringed finger, which he pointed at the ceiling.

"Look at me," he said, "not around the room. You have seen the room before. Look at *me!*"

My eyes felt heavy. I looked at the part in the middle of his wig. My eyes watered and tears ran down my cheeks. I could look no more.

He glanced at the whip that lay coiled beneath his hammock.

"Look at him, dear," Mistress Jenna said.

I lowered my eyes. I looked straight into his. It was like looking at the blazing sun.

"Good," Master van Prok said. "Now tell me what the drums talk about."

They boomed loud now that he had stopped pacing the floor. To the south a third drum had joined in.

"They talked noise and nonsense," I said. "Now they are talking about the day the revolt begins."

Mistress Jenna raised herself in the hammock

and put her feet on the floor. "The day? When is that?"

"The drums don't say when."

A small gasp caught in Mistress Jenna's throat. She flung herself back in the hammock. I felt sorry for her, she looked so pale and frightened.

Master van Prok said, "Gardelin's laws, once the runaways think about them for a day or two, will cool them down. They'll think twice before they attack the plantations."

Mistress Jenna stared at the ceiling as I fanned her.

"I'll send you to St. Thomas. You'll feel better there," Master van Prok said gently.

"And leave you here alone?"

"Only for a month or two. By then the drums will be quiet and you can come home," he promised.

"A month is such a long time."

"You have been starving, Jenna, spending sleepless nights. I worry about you."

"I am worried about you, my dear Jost. I wish you could go to St. Thomas, too. But of course you can't. What awful times have befallen us."

A fourth drum, a small one over the hills to the northeast, was talking now.

Mistress Jenna asked for a drink of rum and I brought it. Kill Devil was all that we had left. She sipped it for a while. Her face brightened.

Suddenly she nudged my foot and told me to pack her things. "Four dresses for daytime," she said. "Three for evening. That is all. I plan to be quiet."

I caught my breath at the thought of leaving St. John.

"And start packing soon," she said. "We don't know when the governor will leave."

She had heard me catch my breath.

"Don't fret," she said. "You'll have more to eat on St. Thomas. You'll like that, won't you, Angelica?"

I was careful not to make her suspicious, to let her know that I would never leave St. John. They could put me in the black hole under the mill and burn me with red-hot pincers.

"I'll pack your clothes tomorrow," I said.

Past midnight, after the van Proks were asleep, Dondo followed me outside. "I heard you talking to Mistress Jenna," he said. "Did you lie when you let her know that you'd go with her?"

"Yes."

"You're not going?"

"No."

"What can you do?"

"Run."

"Where?"

"I don't know. I can't go to Mary Point. Not now. But Whistling Cay is just opposite the point and close. What do you think?"

"I was there once. Caves and places to hide in. They'd never find you."

Nero stood half-hidden in the mill doorway, watching us. Without another word, we parted.

16

Toward evening Gardelin's red-coated soldiers rode into Hawks Nest. They brought the governor bad news. Most of the plantations had missing slaves. Some had lost two slaves. Erik van Slyke at Hurricane Hole had lost four slaves.

One of his runaways had been caught hiding in a tree. He was very young, younger than I, no more than a boy, with scars from two-pronged pincers. Governor Gardelin had him put into the black cave under the sugar mill. The cave was too small to lie down in and the only air came through a crack in the door.

The slaves were called in from the fields. Mistress Jenna and Master van Prok watched from the courtyard. Dondo and I watched from the house, from a window covered with pinguin thorns.

Governor Gardelin gave a speech about runaways. What a crime it was to leave your master who had paid good rigsdalers for you, who fed and housed and protected you.

Raising his voice so that not a single word would be missed, he said, "This man who ran away from Erik van Slyke's plantation was gone longer than three days, longer than five days, longer than seven days. He was gone eight days. Therefore he shall be punished under Article Five of the new laws. He shall receive one hundred and fifty lashes, given to him by Nero, your respected bomba."

There was no sound from the slaves. No sound from the black hole.

Dondo said, "I know this boy. He's called Leander by the whites. I don't know his name. You'll remember the time I was sent to the van Slyke plantation?"

"I don't remember."

"Well, I was sent there by Master van Prok to bring back a child he had bought. The mother didn't want the girl to leave. When Leander and I came to her hut, she set it on fire. I stood there and could not move, as if I was bound with chains. Leander pulled me out of the way. He rushed through the flames and saved the mother but not the child. I remember him well."

The drums had started up and were talking back and forth. Not yet about the boy Governor Gardelin was about to punish.

"One hundred and fifty lashes," Dondo said to me, "will strip the flesh from half his bones. If the boy lives he will be a cripple."

Governor Gardelin said, "I will return tomorrow at noon to see that my orders are promptly carried out."

Before the governor went back to the ship, Isaak Gronnewold talked to him. I was too far away to hear what they were saying, but I saw the governor shrug his shoulders and turn away.

Dondo said quietly, "The boy shall not be punished."

"Be careful, " I warned him. "Soldiers are camped close by. And the bomba will be on the prowl."

"The boy shall not be punished," Dondo said again.

The van Proks came and he said no more.

I brought Mistress Jenna a drink of Kill Devil. As she sipped it, she said to her husband, "He's such a young man. It's a shame to punish him so much. You could purchase him from van Slyke and speak to Governor Gardelin. Perhaps the governor would relent since you wish to use the boy here at Hawks Nest."

"I do not have the money even if his owner wishes to sell him," Master van Prok said. "As for the governor, he is a man who does not relent."

Dondo glanced at me and made a sign that meant the boy was safe. He would not be punished. Making a sign back, I warned him yet again to be careful.

Mistress Jenna drank two more Kill Devils before I put her in bed. She was happy about going to St. Thomas. The governor had told her that he was leaving tomorrow after the boy was punished.

It was midnight when I left her and went outside. A moon among some slow-moving clouds made light shadows everywhere. The drums had picked up the happening at Hawks Nest. The soldiers were playing at cards, shouting and laughing as Dondo left the house.

He passed me without a word. He walked fast to the black hole and lifted the iron rod that barred the door. He pulled the boy out of the hole. He pointed to the north and said, "Run!"

The boy raced by me. I think he was dazed. "Run," I said, "run up the shore to the camp of runaways. It's about . . ." He was gone before I finished.

Dondo had disappeared. I heard Nero scuttling along far up the trail on his midnight prowl. I went to the storehouse and filled a gourd with muscovado. The brown sugar would last me for days.

I hurried halfway up the trail and hid in the cactus by the big tree and waited for Nero to pass on his way back to the tower.

He took a long time. I needed to start for Whistling Cay before the tutu called the slaves to work.

81

I began to worry. Had he seen the boy? Had he seen Dondo? Was he following them? I had to leave before dawn. In the daylight it would be dangerous.

I listened for the noises Nero always made as he shuffled along. A dry wind was blowing down from the hills, rustling the leaves of the mimosa. There were soft, drawn-out sounds from the sea, all kinds of sly sounds, but not the bomba's footsteps.

Suddenly, on the trail between me and the huts, a shot rang out. It was followed by a second shot and a muffled cry. A torch flared through the trees.

I dropped the muscovado and ran. Around a bend in the trail I came upon the bomba. In one hand he held a branch of torchwood, in the other hand, a musket. On the ground in front of him lay a figure crouched in pain.

The boy had escaped. A musket shot had struck Dondo below the knee. It had gone through his flesh but not the bone; still it had brought him down.

The bomba strutted around, muttering threats. He thrust the torch at Dondo's face. "You will pay for this, you scoundrel," he shouted.

Men came. They carried Dondo back to his hut. We bound up the wound and I got some malaguette from the house. As I was giving him the medicine, my hand touched a small packet he had hidden in his hair. It was the gunpowder, the last powder he planned to take.

He fell asleep. The bomba and Master van Prok stood nearby. I slipped the packet into my own hair and hid it under my sleeping mat with the pot fish net. Then I went back to Dondo's hut and stayed with him the rest of the night.

17

The news reached Governor Gardelin soon after dawn. At noon he was at Master van Prok's door. I expected to see him in a fury, but he was calm and smiling, as if he had come to pay a friendly visit.

The two men sat on the porch looking at the blue sea. They drank two mugs of beer, smoked their long-stemmed pipes, and talked. The governor asked about Dondo.

"He's a stout young man and the wound's not serious," Master van Prok said. "He should be around by tomorrow or the next day."

"You mean he will be walking?" the governor asked.

"Limping," the Master said.

"Limping or not, I'll be back to see him," the governor said.

An evil look cast a shadow over his face. Again, he sent for the captain of his small army and told him to visit all the nearby planters as he had the first day, to see that they and three of their slaves were on hand at noon of the following day.

He and Master van Prok drank another mug of beer and talked about the clouds that were gathering in the west. Then he left and returned to his ship, with a happy smile.

He was back in the morning with a long line of sailors, who sang as they climbed the trail from the beach. They had baskets of food, as much food as on the first day. At the end of the line they carried a curious thing of wood and wheels. Never in my life I had seen anything like it. It turned out to be a rack, a thing that pulls people apart.

The field slaves did not go to work that day. After a handful of dried pot fish, the bomba marched them and their children to the tower and had them stand with their backs against the stone wall until the sun went down.

We were quiet through the night. We had slept fitfully. Fear was in the air, in the wind that swept down from the hills, in the poor earth that was sad and packed beneath us. What the governor would do during the coming day no one knew or could guess. But we were sure that it would be bad.

Two of the youngest girls came and lay down beside me. I held their hands and talked to them about the time when rain would fall and flowers bloom.

Soldiers were lined up on both sides of the slaves. The owners of ten plantations sat on benches in front of the tower. Their bombas crouched behind them, and their slaves were gathered with our slaves. Mistress Jenna looked out from the window barred with pinguin thorns, at her husband and Governor Gardelin.

They stood at the cave door where Dondo was locked in. They watched a man who was tinkering with the rack's straps and wheels. I had not seen him before. He had a scraggly gray beard and his chest was covered with a mat of gray hair. He had curly gray hair on the backs of his hands and he was part white.

Governor Gardelin spoke to him. "When, my trusted executioner, will you be ready?"

"I am ready now," the man said. "I have been ready for a long time."

"Good," the governor said.

The locked door was opened and Dondo was pulled out of the cave. It took him a while to stand up.

"You know why you will be punished?" Governor Gardelin asked.

Dondo straightened his shoulders, took a deep breath, and was silent.

"Answer me," the governor said quietly, "or it shall go doubly hard with you."

Still Dondo was silent.

"Look at me respectfully and answer," Governor Gardelin said.

Dondo looked beyond him at the sea and the dark clouds above it and said nothing. He stood with his wounded leg bent. He was in pain but tried not to show it.

"Very well," the governor said, "since you choose to remain silent, whether from stupidity or arrogance, I shall tell the gathering why you are being punished. You have helped a felon to escape. You have tried to escape yourself. These are crimes that insult God and myself, Philip Gardelin, governor of St. Thomas and St. John, chief of the Danish West India and Guinea Company."

He glanced at the fire burning against the wall, where long-handled pincers were heating. He nodded to slaves, who fastened Dondo hand and foot to the trunk of a tree that grew beside the tower door. He made a sign to the executioner. The man drew the pincers from the fire, spat upon them, I guess to test the heat, then put them back in the fire to heat some more.

Isaak Gronnewold rode into the courtyard while the governor was talking. He sat listening until the talk was finished. Then he got down from his donkey and went up to the governor. He was covered with white dust from the trail.

Angry at what he had heard, he stood with his back to the tongs heating in the fire.

"How do you know that Abraham helped the boy escape?" he said. "How do you know that Abraham tried to escape?"

The governor was surprised that anyone would dare to criticize him. His white wig had tilted to one side. He set it carefully on his head and did not answer.

"There has to be a trial, a regular trial," Isaak Gronnewold said. "A man can't be punished for a crime someone decides he has done."

"Someone?" the governor asked. "It's not just someone who has decided. It's the governor of St. Thomas and St. John, the chief of the Danish West India and Guinea Company, who has decided."

Preacher Gronnewold turned to the plantation owners seated on the bench. "What do you say?" he shouted. "Should Abraham be tried?"

"No," Erik Peter van Slyke shouted.

"No," Master van Prok shouted.

A chorus of "nos" rang out. The bombas joined their masters. Our slaves huddled against the stone wall were silent.

"See," the governor said, "you're wrong. Those who struggle to save their fields and mills, who live day and night in constant fear of their lives, say 'no' to you."

Isaak Gronnewold stared at the plantation owners and the bombas, then at the governor.

"They live in terror because their slaves live in terror," Gronnewold said.

He squared his bony shoulders. He stared at Governor Gardelin. He stared at the plantation owners and the bombas. "The Lord has said, 'Inasmuch as ye have done *it* unto one of the least of these my brethren, ye have done *it* unto me.' "

The governor curled his lips.

"And the Lord," Preacher Gronnewold said, "will punish you."

The governor gave him a cold look. "And you will be punished with the iron if you do not cease your chatter."

He turned to the executioner. "You have much to do," he said, "so set about it."

The man took the tongs from the fire. They were a glowing white. He didn't need to spit on them. He began with Dondo's naked feet. There was a faint crackling sound and wisps of smoke rose up. Dondo's legs strained against the ropes that bound him but he did not open his eyes or cry out.

The executioner got ready to clasp his ankles between the pincers. With a shout of "Enough!" Isaak Gronnewold lunged forward and grasped his arms. The man pushed him aside, then knocked him down with a single blow. Soldiers picked him up and carried him to the house, where Mistress Jenna opened the door and let them in.

With one brief glance the executioner measured the size of Dondo's chest. He opened the pincers to fit the size he had measured. With a grunt, he clamped them shut, one tong on each side of Dondo's bare chest. Then he opened the pincers, put them back in the fire, and stood with his arms crossed.

Now there was the odor of roasted flesh on the wind. Excited talk came from the row of plantation owners. Their bombas giggled. Bomba Nero clapped his hands. The governor and Master van Prok exchanged smiles. Mistress Jenna left the window. Our slaves turned their backs, their tongues stiff in their mouths, stiff as mine.

Governor Gardelin spoke to his executioner, who still stood with his arms crossed. "Since we have just begun, let us move along," he said.

The man got out his flogging whip and snapped it a couple of times, first at a flying gull.

"No," the governor said. "The rack before the whip suits us better."

The man gave the rack a glance, turned one of its many wheels, and said, "I am ready, governor, when you are."

"Ready," said Governor Gardelin.

Soldiers untied Dondo. To the governor's surprise, but not to mine, Dondo moaned once and collapsed in the ropes that bound him.

"Wake him," said the governor.

The executioner picked up a handy bucket of seawater and threw it over Dondo's body. The salt and the water did nothing. The governor asked for a second bucket.

Dondo's eyes were closed from the beginning. I believe that his ears were closed, too. He had not heard the talk and the laughter and the crackling fire. He had heard only the big drum at Mary Point. He was not with us anymore. He was back among the green hills of Africa.

18

Mistress Jenna was trying to put medicine down Isaak Gronnewold's throat when I rushed into the house to tell him that Dondo was dead. She had him on the porch where there was some wind from the sea for him to breathe. His face was pale and swollen but his eyes showed fire.

He got to his feet at the news of Dondo's death and staggered outside.

I started to follow him. Mistress Jenna called me back.

"Are your things together?" she said. "The governor is leaving this afternoon."

"Yes," I said, telling her the truth. In my hut under the mat I had the gunpowder I had taken from Dondo, and the net to catch pot fish. I needed a small sack of muscovado, a bush knife, not too large, and tinder, tinder especially, for a fire. There were other things I could use, a pan to cook in and salt, but there was no way I could get either one.

"Do not stop to hear the preacher and Governor

Gardelin argue," she said. "Get your things to-gether and come back. Do not tarry."

And the two men were arguing. They stood face to face at the sugar mill, the governor stiff as a poker and Preacher Gronnewold flailing the air with his bony arms. Master van Prok was listening to them. Nero was talking to the executioner, who was explaining how the straps and wheels worked on the rack that pulled people apart.

I slipped past them without being seen. The mill was deserted. It hadn't made sugar since August, and it was now November. There were four pieces of tinder, one for each of the big kettles. I took the smallest, hid it in my hair, and left.

Nero and the executioner were still talking. I went to the cave where the soldiers had laid Dondo and said goodbye to him. Then I walked past the two men. When I was out of sight I ran.

Our slaves were back in the fields. I picked up a bush knife in one of the huts. It had a broken han-dle and a dull edge, but it was the only small knife I could find. I took the necklace, all the things I had hidden, wrapped them in a goatskin sack and my sleeping mat, balanced the mat on my head, and started for Whistling Cay.

There were two trails, one the white people used and the secret trail that Konje used. I knew where the secret trail started, but it wound back and forth and doubled back on itself, from what he had told me. I could get hopelessly lost.

I took the trail the white people used and went fast, stopping only to listen for donkey hoofs on the stony ground. At Cinnamon Bay I heard voices. It was three slaves carrying casks of seawater up from the shore. I hid in the bushes until they were gone.

At Maho Bay I came upon two white boys playing with a dog. They paused to glance at me and one of them asked whose slave I was. I didn't answer him. The other boy said that I looked like a runaway. Then both of them ran toward a house sitting up on a hill among some trees.

I went faster now and didn't stop until I reached Francis Bay. There I left the trail and followed the shore until I came to a place close to Whistling Cay where the sea was shallow. I waded out to my shoulders, then I had to swim for a short way. I didn't worry about the gunpowder and muscovado. They were wrapped tight in the goatskin sack.

The water was as clear as the air. I could see bottom and hundreds of bright little fish. A school of stingrays — at least twenty of them, with their gray-green eyes that stuck up on small stalks — swam along beside me. Like guides, as if they knew where I was going.

There was no beach where I landed. I had to scramble up one coral ridge after another to reach a level place. From here I could see the cliff at Mary Point rising straight up from the shore.

At the top of the cliff, which was the color of

fresh blood, was a grove of palm trees. In their midst were huts, thatched with palm leaves. People moved about among the trees.

This was the camp of the runaways. This was the camp that Konje ruled. I imagined I saw him. And toward dusk as a big fire started and people began to sing, I imagined that I heard his booming voice rise up above all the other voices, up and up to the stars.

19

Night was coming fast. Higher up lay another ridge of coral. Between it and where I stood was a small valley. You could throw a stone from one side to the other. Trees were growing there that would give me shelter from the hot land wind that had begun to blow.

In the darkness, I made my way through clumps of cactus to the bottom and spread my mat among the trees. The big drum at Mary Point had started to talk, but the rattling leaves and the shrieks that came from the caves drowned out all of the words.

The wind died during the night. The sun rose in a cloudless sky. I was amazed to find that I was surrounded by fruit trees. Long ago, it seemed, when heavy rains fell, water had collected in the meadow and made soil where birdborne seeds could grow.

I jumped to my feet and looked about at my little kingdom. I counted two coconut trees with clusters of nuts hanging from them, a banana tree with a bunch of green, finger-length bananas, and a breadfruit tree bearing six shriveled fruit. There was enough fruit to last for a month.

Against the far side of the valley, on a flat place in the coral, I found African writings, symbols of the Aminas tribe. My idea about the fruit trees being planted by nature could be wrong. Runaway slaves might have lived here years ago and planted them.

Water I had worried about. I could gather wood to build a fire to boil seawater, but I had nothing to collect the steam and let it form into water I could drink.

I needn't have worried. Organ cactus and Turk's head cactus grew everywhere on the slopes around the meadow. After the spines were cut off or burned off and the cactus split open, there was water hidden away in the pulp. You would chew it and the water would seep out. Although it tasted like cooked feathers, still it quenched your thirst.

A thought took my breath away. As I looked around at the fruit trees and the cactus, I saw that I would have enough to live on for weeks. With the fish I caught there would be more than enough.

I could not go to Mary Point, or so Konje had told me over and over, because they suffered from lack of food. If I lived on fruit and cactus and dried the fish I caught and saved it, I could go to Mary

Point. I would have enough food for myself, and for someone else. I would not be a burden on the camp.

That morning I set the fish trap in a pool where the tide flowed in and out and baited it with a sea cucumber. Before noon I had more than a hundred small fish in the trap. They were the length of a finger and if you held one up to the light you could see clear through it. For a meal you had to cook three dozen of them, but they were as good as anything that came from the sea.

I spread the pot fish out on a ledge to dry and covered them with strips of cactus to keep the gulls away, as we did at Hawks Nest. Then I set the trap again, this time in a different place, at the mouth of a cave.

I went into the cave, thinking that it might be a good place to hide if anyone came looking for me.

The opening was narrow for a short distance, then it spread out into a wide room, round in shape, with straight walls. The roof was round also and barely high enough to walk under. In the center of the roof a jagged hole let in a little of the sun so that the room was streaked with moving shadows.

I heard faint sounds, like someone sighing. It was air going through the hole over my head. When the wind blew hard, the sighs could become the deafening shrieks I had heard before.

Beyond this room a passage led on, perhaps into

other rooms. The sun went down while I stood there. I did not stay any longer; but it was a good place to hide if anyone came.

Drums were talking when I got back to the meadow, the big drum at Mary Point, a drum at Maho, and one at Cinnamon Bay.

The big drum still spoke about Dondo's death. But it also spoke something new. In six quick beats and three pauses and six quick beats again, using the name I was known by, it said that I had fled from Hawks Nest and had come to Mary Point.

The big drum lied to encourage other slaves to flee, yet Konje knew that I had fled, that I was hiding somewhere near Mary Point. This made my heart beat fast.

I ate half a breadfruit for supper and thought about eating a few of the fish. At dawn the trap was bulging with twice as many fish as I had taken before. The sun had not found its way through the hole in the roof. But I built a fire there anyway, for fear a fire in the meadow would be seen, and finally ate six of the fish I was saving.

I set the trap again in the same place and carried the fish to the meadow to dry in the sun. The fish I had set out the day before were gone. The gulls had not taken them. I found the tracks of an animal, a strange animal, for there were claw marks in the dust and marks that only something with a long tail could have made.

The loss upset me. It took two days to build a

platform in one of the trees, as high off the ground as I could reach.

The giant lizard with a tail as long as my arm that had taken the fish, that sat watching me from a high ledge during the day, could not climb a tree. The gulls got some of the horde, but still it grew, with more than a hundred fish caught every day at the mouth of the whistling cave.

I didn't keep count of the days. But I guessed from the number of fish I had stored and the news from the big drum that more than a month had passed and it was early December.

The drum urged the slaves to flee the plantations. It talked about the day they would revolt and kill their masters. The day had not been chosen, but it was coming. It was near, the drum said.

In the morning I packed the gunpowder and wrapped the fish in leaves and in the netting I had caught them with, then in my sleeping mat. There were thousands, but they weren't heavy. A dried pot fish is as light as a feather.

The sun was up when I finished. If I started out I could be seen from any of the plantations on Francis Bay. I waited until the next morning, and at dawn, when the first fires burned on the cliff at Mary Point, I got to the beach.

I left the beach before I came to the plantation where I had met the two boys. I saw one of them again but we didn't speak. After a short walk I overtook an old woman carrying a stack of wood on her head. I would have hidden if she had not seen me first.

She greeted me with suspicion. "Where you traveling to?" she asked.

"It's so hot I forget where I am going," I said carefully.

We were near the grove of red-barked turpentine trees Konje had told me about, that marked the trail into Mary Point.

"You got the frightened look," the old woman said. "You're going to the runaway place."

I said nothing.

"Listen, my child. Take my word. Stay away from that place. They're starving. Eating rats and such. Soon they'll be eating each other. When the soldiers come, and they're coming soon, I hear, they'll find you and take you back to the plantation. You know what happens at the plantation."

She drew a finger swiftly across her throat and left me. I couldn't move until she was long out of sight.

20

From the turpentine trees I walked out into a cactus jungle higher than my head. The ground was strewn with spiny clumps. I heard faint voices and someone chopping brush. It was not far to the runaway camp, but there was no sign of a trail.

I balanced the load on my head, pulled my dress tight around me, and took a few steps. They were cautious steps, but cactus spines pierced my feet and I had to stop. There was no way I could get at them unless I returned to where I started.

Under a turpentine tree I put the load on the ground and pulled out the spines. A drop of blood followed them. I wiped the blood away and as I did so, the thud of hoofs came from the stony trail below me. Quickly, I lay flat in the bushes.

Through the trees I saw two donkeys and their riders hurrying up the trail. With them was the boy I had seen on the trail. They came to the trees and stopped. The donkeys were sweating.

One of the men got off. He was white and had a pistol in one hand, his wig in the other, and was sweating like his donkey.

"What do you think?" he said to the other man, who was black.

"I think she got away," the man said.

"She had long legs, longer than yours, Daddy," the boy said. "She ran fast, faster than you did, Daddy. She was gone before you ever told me."

They searched for footsteps. The boy ran up and down. The white man mopped his head and put on his wig.

"She can have gone up the trail to Annaberg," he said.

"No," the black man said. "She didn't go up the trail. Here are her steps. Right here."

They all gazed at the mixed-up footsteps, some that belonged to the boy. They looked out at the spiny forest for a while.

When they had gone I walked toward the sounds the woodchoppers made. I walked sideways, then in a wide circle. I got lost and found a trail, then suddenly I broke out of the jungle into the runaway camp.

Screaming children ran toward me. They were pale under their black skin and their bones stuck out. Certain that I carried food, they would have pulled me down had not the woodchopper scared them with his ax.

At the threats and shouts, Konje ran across the clearing. He lifted me in his arms and put me down.

"What do you bring?" he said.

"Food and some gunpowder."

He grasped the bundle.

"Pot fish. I caught them at Whistling Cay. I caught a lot. Enough to keep me for a long time."

"A long time?" He tore the bundle open and spread the fish on my sleeping mat. "That time is upon us," he said.

He was surrounded now by runaways, by their wives and children. He told them to be quiet. He gave each of them a handful of pot fish.

"Do not eat them today," he said. "Eat them tomorrow. That way tonight you will have food to dream about."

Unhappy sounds came from the throng, but no one ate one fish that day.

I marveled at the way Konje ruled. More than one hundred and fifty runaways lived in the camp. One was a prince from the Gulf of Guinea. Yet Konje's word was law.

He had held the camp together from the beginning, I learned, through days when there was nothing to eat and drink but cactus pulp. Through a time when the prince threatened to leave and take the runaways to a different hideout. Konje had listened to his complaints, then drove him out of Mary Point.

My friend Lenta was here in the camp. She had

fled early from the plantation owned by the two brothers. They had forced themselves upon her and she had run away with her son when the drums first began to talk at Mary Point.

She was a fine cook, as I have said. Konje often came to our home in Barato just to eat her food. Before the day was out he sent me to work for her.

Everyone in the camp had work to do. Some of the women gathered wood. Some kept the fronts of the huts clear and the paths that ran between them, through a field of catch-and-deep, a hooked thorn bush that caught everything it touched, to the rocks at the edge of the cliff.

Others gathered organ cactus, twice as tall as a tall man, and cut it into chunks. It gave us the only water for the camp. Men went down to Maho Bay at night and set traps for pot fish. This was the food we ate most of the time.

More than a hundred of the men had muskets. Before supper that night, by the light of turpentine torches, they drilled at the cactus wall, the only place the plantation owners and the Civil Guard could force their way into the camp. They did not fire their muskets, because gunpowder was scarce, but Konje went up and down the lines and saw that they acted like warriors and not like men out to have a good time.

He sent young men to the cliff to hunt for bird eggs and any birds they could catch. For supper that night Lenta cooked up for the camp two big iron pots of weevily flour, very old sea-bird eggs, and a dozen large birds. She sprinkled handfuls of ground-up kaleloo, a vine that grew everywhere and had a good taste, into the pot. Everyone said it was the best food they had eaten in many days.

While we were eating, drum talk came from the east. The drums wanted to know if Mary Point was ready for an attack. The Civil Guard, thirty of them, had gathered at Duurloo's.

Konje went to the big drum standing in front of the cookhouse — a hollow log with a tight goatskin cover. He sent out word that he was ready but to bring powder to the turpentine trees during the night.

Afterwards little gombee drums were brought out. We sang songs of Africa but did not dance. Beneath the songs were fear and sadness.

21

Drums were talking. The talk came from all directions, from one hill to another. From Hurricane Hole in the east, to Ram's Head, along the coast to Great Cruz Bay, to Little Cinnamon, at last to Duurloo's fort.

Konje said, "There's so much talk it's hard to tell one word from another. It's clear that slaves have revolted at some of the plantations, but where?"

In midmorning more news came. A lone figure stumbled into camp, waving an ironwood club. He wandered to the cooking hut, fell down in the dust, and didn't move until late that day. It was Nero, van Prok's bomba.

He had a flask of Kill Devil rum in his pocket. With it Konje got him to speak. He beat upon the ground with his club, opened his mouth, and made noises. Finally, with the last of the rum inside him, between long pauses he told Konje more about the revolt.

Runaway slaves were moving west from Ram's

Head, moving along the coast toward us, looting and killing as they came. At Duurloo's, his eighty-seven slaves were fighting among themselves. Duurloo had taken his family along with himself to Duurloo Cays.

Governor Gardelin, Nero said, had issued an order giving fifty rigsdalers for every runaway brought in to Duurloo's fort, dead or alive, which meant that dozens of loyal slaves would be searching for runaways, killing them if necessary.

Nero had left van Prok's at dawn. The news he brought was therefore fresh. It was also true, Konje felt, because Nero appeared to have changed his loyalty from the whites to the runaways.

"We can handle the runaways if they come this way," Konje said. "But it's those who are out to collect the fifty rigsdalers we must watch for. It's hard to tell whether a slave is loyal to his master or not."

I glanced at the bomba sitting by the fire with his ironwood club across his knees. It was possible that he was still loyal to Master van Prok. Konje thought so too and kept an eye on him until he went to sleep.

Early in the morning the next day Preacher Gronnewold walked into camp. He had to leave his donkey in the turpentine trees. Behind him he led two goats he had found along the trail. They were not fat and not thin and covered with spines.

Isaak Gronnewold tied them up and spoke to

Konje. "I left Duurloo's this morning at dawn. The Civil Guard is getting ready to attack Mary Point. But not today. Not until they have more powder for their cannon. That's coming from Little Cruz and won't be there until tomorrow."

Nero said, "But look for them tonight."

Konje had come to trust him. His back was covered with puffy, red burns. Van Prok, for a reason Nero never told us, had used red-hot pincers on him.

Konje took Nero's advice and sent a man out to the turpentine trees. If he saw or heard Civil Guards coming up the trail from Duurloo's, the sentry was to give a parrot's ringing squawk.

Late in the afternoon, while the goats were roasting in a pit and most of the camp stood around watching, sniffing in the wonderful smells, we heard a parrot cry. Guards had been sighted. Then there were ten quick cries and two long ones.

Konje doubled the number of cries and said, "Twenty Civil Guards are on the trail, dragging two cannons."

He ordered the women into their huts. Lenta stayed by the pit, behind the stones where the goats were roasting, and I stood beside her. We both had knives.

The men ran for their muskets. Konje divided them into two bands and placed a band at each end of the cactus wall. Behind him he placed men who carried long knives used for cutting sugar cane.

109

We waited. It was almost dusk when the first cannon roared.

"Gardelin has sent them some good powder," Konje said.

A cannonball burst through the wall, sending strips of cactus flying through the air. A second shot widened the gap and sped past our huts toward the cliff.

The path the cannon had made was wide and strewn with thorny chunks. A Civil Guard appeared, far back along the path, slowly picking his way toward us. A musket brought him down. Guards pulled him away and disappeared.

They fired ten more cannon shots that did no harm. No other guards showed themselves along the path, but they yelled at us and said they would return when they had more powder. We did not yell back. Instead we celebrated our victory.

22

While the sun went down, we tasted the good smells from the roasting meat. Everyone sang and danced to the sounds of the gombee drums. Konje and I danced together. For me it was like dancing with the north wind when it blew down from the jungle across Barato and I couldn't breathe.

When the dancing stopped, Konje went to check on his sentry. He thought that the Guards might come back in the dark. While he was gone, I boldly asked Preacher Gronnewold if he would marry us. No matter what happened, we would be together.

After Konje returned, Minister Gronnewold took us by the arms. He told us to hold hands. He opened his Bible. But an odd look came over Konje's face and slowly, he backed away.

"What's wrong?" Isaak Gronnewold asked him.

Konje didn't answer. It seemed that he couldn't think of a word to say.

"In Barato," I explained, "a man can't marry until he's thirty years old. Konje is only twenty-eight."

Preacher Gronnewold laughed. "Listen, young man, you are not in Africa and likely you never will be. Step up here and give me your hand."

Konje still was silent. A crowd of women, who had gathered around us, began to make fun of him. "He looks forty years old," one of them said. "Fifty years old," another said.

I went out and sat down by the fire, far from tears but angry. I turned away from Konje so he couldn't see my face. Suddenly I was swept into the air and whirled around and around. The north wind was blowing through the jungle again.

Isaak Gronnewold smiled and told us to put our hands together. He opened his Bible. He read some words and Konje said something and I said, "Yes."

"You are now man and wife," the preacher told us.

A small silver moon hung low overhead. Streamers of black clouds, rain clouds, hovered around it. A night bird called to its mate and was answered.

"Good omens," Konje said, with a kiss.

Toward dawn, as I lay tight in his arms, I heard a wind in the monkey-pod trees, rattling the pods. Then it was quiet. Then the wind swept down upon the camp, lifting the leaves on the roofs. From Whistling Cay came shrieks and moans that sounded like tortured people.

The sun rose in clouds of fire. The clouds turned black and tumbled across the sky. Gently, it began to rain. Then the rain ceased and started again. By nightfall water was running through the camp, pouring over the cliff in a muddy stream.

It rained for more than a week. The meadow became a lake. The files of cactus, taller than men, turned a bright green. You could feel them drinking up the rain, storing water for the next drought.

The wind never ceased. The moans and shrieks that came from Whistling Cay were so loud that we couldn't tell whether Duurloo's drums were talking or the far-off drums at Little Cruz and Coral Bay.

Konje, sure that his papa drum would be heard despite the wind, sent out messages. They were always the same: "Slaves, we need you at Mary Point. Bring guns, bring food. Do not wait."

A woman came, bringing ten loaves of bread she had baked with stolen flour over a fire in the hills. Two men came with food they had stolen at Great Cruz Bay — hundreds of hard biscuits wrapped in cloth sheets, sheets stained with blood. They also brought news they had gathered along the coast.

The storm had washed cliffs into the sea and destroyed all the trails. Fighting at Great Cruz Bay had stopped. At Duurloo's fort loyal slaves watched the runaways across a wreckage of trees, stone, and mud. The Civil Guards waited for powder from Governor Gardelin in St. Thomas.

Konje had a meeting at suppertime with Isaak Gronnewold and Nero. It was the first time since

I had been in the camp that he had asked for advice. The three of them sat on the ground in front of the cooking hut, eating the daily pot fish.

Konje said, "I hear from the men who brought us fish this morning that the trail from Maho Bay is washed out. When the Civil Guards get their powder from Gardelin and start up the trail with their cannon they'll go no farther than Maho Bay, not until the trail can be used. Which means that we have a few days to get ready for another attack."

Isaak Gronnewold shook his head. "This time they'll come with more men. With more cannon and more powder. If you run them off, if you kill all of them, Governor Gardelin will send more men. He'll not stop until there's not a single runaway left on Mary Point. If by chance he fails, the King of Denmark will send a governor who will not fail."

Konje stared at the preacher. He did not believe what he had heard. "You mean that we should give up and return to the plantations? Have our legs cut off? Have our bones broken with a hammer?"

"No," Isaak Gronnewold said. "I'll go to St. Thomas and talk to the governor. I'll tell him that hundreds will die if the fighting goes on at Mary Point. That you are strong here. That the runaways at Great Cruz Bay are strong. They have already killed planters. It's wise, I will say to him, that the harsh punishments he wrote into law be rewritten so the slaves are treated like humans instead of like beasts of the jungle."

Konje laughed, a bitter laugh that chilled me. He did not answer. He turned to Nero, because the bomba had lived a long time on the island and knew the plantations and their owners.

"Do not stay and wait to be attacked," the bomba said. "If you do, if it takes a month or a year, they'll finally kill everyone on Mary Point. You have more than a hundred men with muskets. Lead them out of this trap and join the runaways at Great Cruz Bay. Together, you can drive every white from the island of St. John."

Konje took his advice. He drilled the men for nearly a month, until the trails could be used. The women were drilled, too. We had cane knives and were taught how to use them.

It was during one of these drills, as the sun came up in a blaze of fire, while I was marching with a knife clasped in my hand, that I decided to tell Konje what I had known for days, that I was carrying his child.

23

Nero's plan, unfortunately, had to wait. At Great Cruz Bay, Prince Tamba, who had been driven from our camp, was having trouble with a Prince Foulah. They had stopped looting and killing whites and were fighting each other.

Konje waited day by day for the fighting to stop. He sent messages on the big drum, urging them to make peace. At last, word came that Prince Foulah had done away with Prince Tamba. He was moving west along the coast to meet Konje and his men at Duurloo's fort.

At this news, Isaak Gronnewold went down to the fort to talk peace before the two men could join their forces. Konje got ready to leave at dusk the next day, skirting Maho Bay and slipping down upon Duurloo's from the hills, hoping to be unseen.

But the next morning, a boy who had gone out to hunt squirrels came running back to camp out of breath. He couldn't speak but he made sounds and pointed toward the cliff.

Konje, still half asleep, stopped combing his hair and gave the boy a shake. Getting no words from him, he took my hand and we went through the meadow, following the boy to the edge of the cliff.

Below us, in the deep water between Whistling Cay and the cliff, lay a great ship. It was not Governor Gardelin's ship or a slave ship like *God's Adventure*. It was twice as big as both of them. It had dozens of guns sticking out from its decks. It had three tall masts and flags fluttering from them all. Men walked the decks in blue uniforms and red wide-brimmed hats.

Konje and I looked at each other, speechless as the boy.

On the ship's stern was a name, painted in gold letters. Three words I had not seen before. I spelled out the letters — R O I D E F R A N C E.

"Do they mean anything to you?" Konje said.

"Nothing," I said.

We soon learned about the ship. Everyone at Mary Point had gathered around us. All had their weapons. Isaak Gronnewold, who had come back from Duurloo's before dawn and had decided not to awaken the camp with the bad news he brought, came and stood on the edge of the cliff, looking down at the beautiful ship. Then he opened his Bible and took out a paper.

"This paper was written by Pierre Dumont, the

captain of the ship that lies below us," he said to Konje. "The paper is written in French. One of Duurloo's slaves, who speaks the language, put it into Danish. It was given to me to give to you."

He looked grim, but none of us who crowded around him expected the awful words that came.

"The paper says that all runaways at Mary Point are to surrender within twenty-four hours and lay down their muskets and knives. If they disobey, they will be returned to their plantations and promptly punished."

"Who are these people who tell us what to do?" Konje said, pale with anger beneath his dark skin.

"Gardelin asked the French who own the island of Martinique for help. He begged them to send one of their warships and end the rebellion. The French are here with three hundred men and fifty cannon."

"We'll turn them back the same way we turned back the Guards," Konje said.

"The French have other ships and other men."

"We'll turn them back also."

"More will come."

"Let them."

The captain's paper fluttered in the wind. Konje reached out and tore it into pieces. The wind carried the pieces over the cliff. A cheer rose from the crowd: "Sno de mun, sno de mun, sno de mun, Français." Slave talk that meant, "Frenchman, shut your mouth."

The words hung in the air for a long time. Nobody put down a knife or a musket.

"Where have the Frenchmen gone?" Konje asked.

"To Duurloo's. It's wise not to wait and fight them here," the bomba said. "Tonight we can take the trail to Water Bay. It's about a mile from here. Hide out for an hour or two. Make sure that the French are still at Duurloo's, then use the trail around van Prok's."

"Van Prok is in St. Thomas with his wife," Konje said.

"Good. We'll go to the plantation, take what food and rum we can find, horses and mules, if any are left, skirt Duurloo's in small groups, not more than ten — and meet Prince Foulah on his way from Great Cruz Bay."

Konje had no chance to answer. Three soldiers came out from the turpentine trees and through the gap the cannon had made. One of the soldiers had a trumpet and one a drum. The soldier in the middle held a white flag tied to a pole. Behind them came a squad of soldiers, armed with swords and muskets.

They marched past our empty huts and down through the meadow. We stood at the edge of the cliff, ready with our weapons, and watched them come.

"What does the white flag mean?" Konje asked Isaak Gronnewold.

119

"It means that they're here to talk peacefully," he explained.

The soldier with the flag stopped in front of them. He wore a blue uniform that was too tight for him and shining boots. On both his cheeks were small red scars.

"Captain Dumont commanded you to lay down your arms," the soldier said. "But here you stand with your culprits, every one of them armed, facing me with arrogant looks."

"We were commanded to lay down our weapons tomorrow," Konje said.

"Captain Dumont has changed his mind."

"Does he change it often?"

"As often as he wishes."

"Mine I do not change," Konje said. "Tomorrow I will give Captain Dumont my answer, not today."

He was fighting for time. He had taken Nero's advice. Tonight he planned to leave the camp, join Prince Foulah, and drive the white people into the sea.

The squad of soldiers began to shuffle their feet.

Aware that it was a dangerous moment, Isaak Gronnewold spoke out. "Where is Captain Dumont?"

"With his army," the soldier said.

"Where is the army?"

"On the island of St. John."

"Will you tell Captain Dumont that I wish to talk to him?"

"Captain Dumont did not come here to talk," the soldier said and nodded to the trumpeter.

24

We stood among the rocks on the edge of the cliff. The sounds of drums and marching feet came closer. Captain Dumont and his army were not far away, between us and Maho Bay.

The soldier raised his voice. "Lay down your knives and muskets."

"No!" Konje shouted. "We do not surrender."

We clutched our weapons.

Among the turpentine trees, through the gap in the cactus, I saw a flash of helmets.

"Captain Dumont and his army are at the gates," the soldier said to Konje. "They'll be here in moments. If you and your people confront them, there'll be trouble. Again I tell you to lay down your weapons."

"I wish to talk to Captain Dumont," Konje said. "After we talk, I will think about the weapons."

He tried to speak in a friendlier way. He must have realized that we were trapped. He had given up all thought of Nero's plan.

The soldier said, "You have heard the orders of Captain Dumont."

One of our men, I believe it was Jacob, who was old and very short-tempered, yelled, "Jeg lugter fisk," Danish for "I smell something fishy."

The soldier dropped the white flag. He took his sword from its sheath and pointed it at Konje. Behind him a musket roared and a shot passed close above Konje's head.

Preacher Gronnewold went to stand between the two men. In an act of friendship, he reached out his hand to touch the soldier. It was a terrible mistake.

Whether from anger or fear, the man drew away. Preacher Gronnewold again put out a friendly hand. Once again a shot rang out. It struck Preacher Gronnewold in the breast and he fell to the ground.

I ran to help him. He struggled to his knees and held the Bible high above his head. "This is the way," he said in a choking voice. "This is the only way!"

The Bible slipped from his hand. He closed his eyes. He stopped breathing. Konje placed his body among the rocks on the edge of the cliff.

I found my knife where I had dropped it in the grass and went and stood with the other slaves. There was not a sound. Silent, we waited for Konje to tell us what to do.

The man with the flag took his soldiers away.

123

We watched them go through the meadow, through the gap in the cactus and disappear.

Konje said, "Soon the French will come. Stay where you are. Do not taunt them. Do not fire on them. First, I'll talk to their captain. If talk fails, then we will do what we must."

25

Clouds streaked the rising sun. A strong wind blew in from the west. Sounds like a great animal breathing rose up from Whistling Cay. Silently, we clutched our weapons and waited for Captain Dumont and his army.

They came with flying flags, to the beat of many drums, through the gap in the wall and past our huts. Halfway through the meadow they stopped.

I counted them. Ten soldiers in a row and more than twenty rows, carrying swords and long-barreled muskets. Other slaves counted them too, for small gasps went up everywhere. I glanced at Konje. His face had not changed. It showed no signs of fear.

Captain Dumont, with an officer at his side, walked forward and stood in front of us. He had a pointed beard that was turning gray. He wore a three-cornered hat and a curly white wig.

"Who is the man called Apollo?" he asked in a brisk voice, speaking Danish well.

"Here I am," Konje said, but he did not move. "Have you come to talk?"

The captain gave a small nod.

"Do we talk as men, one to another," Konje asked, "or do we talk as slave and master?"

"You're a slave, so talk as a slave."

"I will talk as a free man or not at all," Konje said angrily.

"Enough!" Captain Dumont said.

He spoke to the officer beside him, who stepped out to put a chain on Konje's wrists. Without a word, with a single blow, Konje sent him sprawling.

Captain Dumont turned pale. He stared at the officer, then at Konje, but said nothing. The army behind him must not have seen the blow or the officer lying dazed on the ground. There was not a sound from them.

Konje backed away to the very edge of the cliff and stood between two towering rocks. He was no longer angry. He glanced at Captain Dumont in his three-cornered hat and curly wig. At the captain's shining soldiers that covered the meadow.

His eyes fell for a moment upon us, huddled silently together, clutching our knives and muskets. There was a look on his face I had never seen before. As if he were high in the heavens. As if he were God looking down upon his people.

I watched him look for a time at the waves washing over the rocks far below us. I watched him draw back from what he saw.

126

Nero, who stood beside me, said, "Why does he stand there? What is he waiting for? There's fighting and dying to be done."

Konje raised his musket and pointed it at Captain Dumont. Then he flung it on the ground and told us to do the same with our weapons.

"We do not honor you with a battle," he said to the captain. "Nor do we surrender."

Captain Dumont did not answer. He didn't move when our weapons clattered to the ground, when Nero held tight to his ironwood club. He seemed not to believe what had happened before his eyes.

Konje came and took Nero back to the edge of the cliff. They talked for a moment, bracing themselves against the wind that threatened to sweep them away.

For a while they were silent, gazing out at the sea and the far horizon. Then Nero flung his club at the French army. In one leap, he was in the air, falling toward the rocks below.

"Like Nero, it is time for all to go," Konje said. "To leave this brutal bondage."

"Yes, yes," slaves shouted.

"And go away to greener shores and freedom."

"Yes, yes, yes."

I heard no moans and saw no tears, though it was clear to everyone by now what we were to do.

Five girls came. They put their arms around each other and leaped, singing a joyful song. I heard their voices for a long time.

Old Jacob came out of the crowd. He shouted an insult at Captain Dumont, brandished his walking club, and was gone. My friend Lenta waved to me. She had her son by the hand. He looked frightened and held back, but she swept him in her arms, and they too were gone. Men and women swarmed over the cliff.

The French sailors in their bright blue jackets leaned quietly on their shining muskets. Captain Dumont watched with his arms crossed upon his chest. I believe he was glad that the slaves were leaping to their deaths, that he would not have the trouble of taking them back to the plantations, to be pinched with hot irons and to have their legs cut off.

Clouds hid the sun. Sea hawks hovered in the gray air. Our people had gone. Konje and I were alone.

He held out his strong hands and I went toward him. But I took only a few steps. Suddenly, slowly, for the first time, I felt our child stir. I stopped and braced myself against the wind.

"What's wrong?" Konje said.

"Nothing," I answered.

"It's something." He looked down at me with his burning eyes. "The child?"

"Yes."

"Don't think of the child, for we all go together—the three of us, to a better world and happier days."

"Happy days will soon be here."

"Never, not on this island. Come, it's time to leave."

"No," I said.

He grasped my hands. I thought he meant to drag me over the cliff. I did not move. I could not move. A stricken look crossed his face and he backed away. He stood among the rocks on the edge of the cliff, but in a moment he was gone. The gray sky enclosed him. I ran to the cliff, praying that I had dreamed an awful dream.

From far below rose a faint sound. I imagined that it was his voice calling to me. I took one heavy step, but my body stirred again. And I moved no farther. Our child bound me to the earth that I stood upon, bound me to life forever.

Afterword

When Captain Dumont learned that Jost van Prok had fled the day before his home burned to the ground, he took Raisha to the French island of Martinique. Here she worked in his household, caring for his children. Her daughter was born some months later. After a year, under the French laws, she was no longer a slave. She was free and her daughter was free.

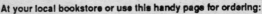